Love Stories

At First Sight

Elizabeth Chandler

D1636205

BANTAM BOOKS
NEW YORK • TORONTO • LONDON • SYDNEY • AUCKLAND

For Jenny and Jessica,
shining more brightly each year.

RL 6, age 12 and up

AT FIRST SIGHT

A Bantam Book / November 1998

Produced by 17th Street Productions,
a division of Daniel Weiss Associates, Inc.
33 West 17th Street
New York, NY 10011.
Cover photography by Michael Segal.

ISBN: 0-553-49254-3

Published simultaneously in the United States and Canada

Bantam Books are published by Bantam Books, a division of Bantam
Doubleday Dell Publishing Group, Inc. Its trademark, consisting of the
words "Bantam Books" and the portrayal of a rooster, is Registered in
U.S. Patent and Trademark Office and in other countries. Marca
Registrada. Bantam Books, 1540 Broadway, New York, New York 10036.

PRINTED IN THE UNITED STATES OF AMERICA

OPM   0 9 8 7 6 5 4 3 2 1

One

"IF YOU PUT off leaving much longer," Miss Henny said to me, "it'll be dark before you arrive in New York."

I peered through the lace curtains of her little stone house at the edge of Fields's campus. Christmas was four days away. My silver Audi was out front, packed with gifts and sports stuff, videos and books, enough to keep me occupied during the long winter vacation.

Miss Henny sipped her tea, studying me. "I believe you'd be more eager to set off with a tent and team of dogs for Christmas in northern Alaska."

"I have a tent. Do you know where I can get some dogs?"

She laughed in that gay, ladylike way of hers that seemed to belong to another era. "Be sure to send my love to Sandra and Julia."

I nodded and drained my cup of tea, the third or

1

fourth I had drunk. Sandra and Julia were my beautiful sisters, twins a year younger than I, who until last year had boarded with me at Fields School in Maryland. Because of our father's job with a mining company, our parents had moved from one foreign city to another. They lived in some pretty exotic locations, but none of them were exactly good places to raise three girls. So for our middle- and high-school years, we were sent to Fields. Then last summer, when our parents came back to the States for good, my sisters bolted for what they considered a "normal" school—the coed public school in the tiny town of Thornhill, New York—our new home.

I'd chosen to finish my senior year at Fields, which to me felt more like home than anywhere else. My sixth-grade teacher, Miss Henny, had become more than an instructor. Over the years she was the one who kept us at her house when the airport was fogged in, who picked us up when we arrived back early from holidays, and who gave us tea and tissue and sympathy when we got the flu. As for the school itself, I loved it. I played on several teams, enjoyed the strong academics, and had a great group of friends. There was only one thing Fields was missing—guys. Not that it really mattered. Unlike that of my popular sisters, my love life was sure to be nonexistent no matter what.

"Allison," Miss Henny said. She always called me by my full name when she was about to say something important. "You know how every New Year's Eve I have a wish for you? Since I won't be seeing you till the term begins, I'll give it to you now."

"Okay." *New Year's Eve,* I thought. There were certain times of the year when my sisters' dating schedule could be tracked only by a computer with extensive memory. Even at Fields their romantic life was legendary. At prom time they'd had so many guys interested in them that they negotiated blind dates for me and almost half my classmates. It was as if the school had put up double radio towers from their dorm rooms, sending out waves to the all-male school three miles away. Now, according to my mother's letters, the twins had taken Thornhill's dating scene by storm. I was dreading having to be the boring, plain-looking sister standing on the sidelines once again. In the small town, where everybody knew one another, the holidays would be full of parties, Mom wrote, "with lots of cute boys for you to meet." That's my mother, ever hopeful.

"My wish," Miss Henny said, breaking into my thoughts, "is that you finally realize all you have to offer others."

"But I do already," I protested. "Fields has been teaching self-esteem since I got here." Hammering it into our heads, actually.

"Then let me be more specific. My wish is that you realize how easy it would be for a nice young man to fall in love with you."

I stared at the thin, gray-haired lady who had never married.

"Your sisters have their beauty; you have yours."

I blinked. How did she know?

3

"Time for you to go," my old teacher said, taking my cup from me and gently pulling me up from the chair. "Don't you have a dinner invitation from your aunt Jen tonight?"

I nodded and put on my jacket. It was the one part I always liked about holidays, seeing my unpredictable godmother.

"I'll miss you terribly, dear. Come back with some good stories." Miss Henny wrapped a wool scarf around my neck and laid her hand lightly against my cheek.

Somehow, without realizing it, I'd grown several inches taller than she. Now she seemed so fragile, like one of her dainty porcelains. Thinking about how she'd aged, I got a lump in my throat. I was halfway down the stone path, lost in dismal thoughts of happy school years slipping away from me, when Miss Henny called out with the howl of a college football coach, "Go get 'em, Al!"

Two hours later I was buzzing up the New Jersey Turnpike, singing Christmas carols along with the radio, when I suddenly realized just how much tea I had drunk at Miss Henny's. I don't know who lays out highways, but it seems they always put rest stops nineteen miles past the moment you figure out you need one—and need it *now*.

I picked up speed. I was close to desperate when I finally hit the exit ramp to the rest stop. By the time I'd circled the jammed lot twice and squeezed my car into a parking space, I was beyond desperate.

I raced across the asphalt, up the steps, and through the glass doors. The foyer was crowded with holiday travelers, and I made the sidesteps and spins of an NFL running back to get to the rest-room area.

Bam! Two other people were also trying to get there, and we all smashed into each other. The three of us spun around like revolving doors—a tall guy, a little boy, and me.

"Whoa!" The guy held the kid and me as we whipped around.

"Sorry!" said the little boy.

"No problem," I responded.

The little boy rushed headlong toward one bathroom entrance and I toward the other.

"Hold up there," the guy called after us.

The kid and I both looked back at him. He was about my age and had dark hair—that's all I had time to notice. He pointed to the signs above the doors, then crossed his hands.

I glanced up at the stick figure of a man. "Whoops." The kid and I crossed paths, each of us finally making it to our right destination.

On my way back out of the ladies' room I glanced at myself in the mirror and saw that my short brown hair had become electric with winter dryness, silky pieces of it flying about. I guess the self-consciousness I always felt when standing next to my gorgeous sisters was already beginning. I frowned at the oval reflection of my face, my lips and deep brown eyes, entirely bare of makeup, suddenly looking very plain. As usual I had nothing but a comb and lip gloss in my bag. I wet down my hair, flattening it against my head, and left.

As I got in line for pizza I thought about delicate Miss Henny bellowing out, "Go get 'em, Al!" I guess I was smiling, for I suddenly noticed the person in front of me watching my face and smiling back.

"Hi," he said. He had beautiful hazel eyes that could melt a girl. Okay, so he was a little short to take to a prom—he was very cute and the right height for a first or second grader. "Did you make it in time?" the little boy asked me.

"Yup. How about you?"

"Just in," he replied.

The guy who was with him, the one who had directed us to the right rooms, turned around. He was tall and had brown eyes with an almost golden light in them, eyes equally capable of turning a girl to syrup. His easy smile told me he knew it. "Close call," he said.

I nodded and smiled a little, feeling awkward around this hunk of a guy, wondering what to say next.

My sisters would've known. Once when they were still at Fields, they gave a flirting seminar in the dorm. It was the most well-attended extracurricular we'd ever had. They demonstrated things like tilting your head and saying something clever, playing off whatever line the guy has just fed you. They spoke in depth about using your eyes to give meaning to what you're saying—you know, flashing them or raising an eyebrow or whatever.

Easy for the twins to say! When Sandra tilts her

6

head, her streaky blond hair tumbles a little farther down one perfect shoulder. When I try it, with my short, wispy hair, I look like an inquisitive bird. Besides, how do you play off a line like "Close call"? *Yeah, I was never so glad to see an empty stall.*

"Did you wash your hair?" the little boy asked.

My hand flew up to my head.

"That's the style, Tim," the older guy said. "She used mousse."

Tim studied my head with interest.

"Actually," I told Tim, "I just wet it down, trying to keep myself from looking like a mad scientist with a short circuit."

Tim enjoyed my explanation. "Like Doctor Fuzzbuzz," he said.

"Old Porcupine Head," I replied.

"Ms. Fizzy Wig."

"No, no," I said, with mock seriousness, "she's the assistant."

Tim found this incredibly funny. I found Tim, with his mop of light brown hair and dusting of freckles, incredibly charming. "You're pretty," Tim said.

I tilted my head. "You say that to all the girls."

"Just the ones I like." His eyes were round and innocent. This kid was destined to break a lot of girls' hearts. "Would you buy me an ice cream?" he asked. "My brother won't."

I glanced up at Tim's brother, one eyebrow raised. He gave me the exact same look back.

I turned to Tim. "What's *he* got against ice

7

cream?" I asked. Out of the corner of my eye I saw his brother checking me out, his gaze slowly sweeping down and up me. I turned to face him. He laughed, not at all self-conscious about being caught in the act, holding my eyes with his.

Whoa, I thought, *I've been flirting!* Mostly with a seven-year-old, of course, and maybe that's why it seemed so easy. But the guy had noticed. And immediately the old, uncomfortable feelings began to creep in. I wished my sisters were there to pick up the conversation and bail me out.

Then the guy said, "My name is Ben. And what I've got against ice cream is that it becomes liquid. Immediately. We can't stop at every bathroom. I told Tim to choose between a small soda and an ice cream."

It was hard to take my eyes from his—he had the absolute confidence to gaze back at me without blinking.

"I'd suggest the same thing for you," he added, smiling.

"I'm taller than Tim. I can have twice as much."

Ben laughed.

"Want to share a pizza with us?" Tim asked.

"I—uh—"

"Not if she's going to eat twice as much as you," Ben said to his brother.

"I'll pay for my own," I assured him.

"Will you pay for ours too?" Ben asked. "I think you're onto a good thing, Tim. Every rest stop we'll pick up a hot girl and—"

A hot girl? I must've gotten a funny expression

on my face because Ben then touched me lightly on the elbow and said, "Just kidding. *I'll* pay if you'd like to join us."

"Dutch treat," I replied, amazing myself by accepting the invitation.

But then, why not? This might not happen again for another five years, unless, of course, I started frequenting rest stops. Plus I was sure I'd never see Ben again. I could act however I wanted, and who would know? If I made an idiot of myself, I'd never have to face him again. The realization was incredibly freeing.

"What's your name?" Ben asked.

"Allie."

"Allie Cat!" Tim crowed.

I smiled at him.

"Do you like pepperoni, Cat?" Tim asked.

"Anything but anchovies."

"How about goldfish?" Tim asked.

"Only if they're salted."

Tim thought this was hilarious. We finally settled on pepperoni with extra cheese. I forced a couple of dollars into Ben's hand, then Tim and I nabbed a table.

He and I told knock-knock jokes till Ben brought over the pizza and sodas. As we munched we talked about movies, sports, and the gifts Tim hoped he would get for Christmas. Eventually I learned that their parents had divorced last year and the boys were on the way to visit their father.

"And his fiancée. Can't wait to meet the woman," Ben said, grimacing.

The look on his face made me reluctant to ask any other questions related to home. And the truth was, I didn't feel like delving into my family situation either. I did mention Fields.

"A girls' boarding school?" Ben said with surprise. "No guys?"

"A lot of guys—three miles away."

Ben thought for a moment. "I guess that makes it a lot harder to date."

"Not for me," I said jauntily. It was the truth—three miles was no harder than three feet away—it all seemed pretty impossible to me.

"Really," he said, interpreting my statement in a different way, smiling and studying me. "Well, at least it cuts down on distractions."

I raised my eyebrows, hoping I looked interested and beguiling rather than bug-eyed. "Do you have trouble concentrating?"

"Right now?" he asked back.

I blushed and he laughed, winning that round. Then Tim volunteered, "Ben has trouble concentrating on one girl."

"Thanks, Tim," Ben said. It was my turn to laugh. One side of Ben's mouth drew up. "You find that funny?"

"No, no," I said. What was funny was that I, Allison Parker, was trying to flirt with a pro.

When we'd finished the last bit of crust, we gathered our trash and walked slowly out to the parking lot.

"Where's your car?" Ben asked.

I pointed across the lot.

"This is ours," Tim said proudly, resting his hand on an ancient red Toyota.

"Now you know why I don't want to stop too often," Ben said to me. "I'm afraid it won't start again."

"Do you want me to stay and make sure you get back on the road?" I offered.

"No thanks. Tomato Soup hasn't let us down yet."

I smiled. Tomato soup was an exact description of the car's color.

"Well, it's been nice meeting you," I said, shaking his hand. Ben held on until I looked into his eyes. Until that moment I had no idea that looking and touching could be so dangerous. I felt light-headed and tingly all over. Withdrawing my hand, I quickly backed away and saw a smile touch his lips. He was used to girls responding to him like that. He counted on it. And I was sure that I'd just given myself away as a blushing amateur.

Fortunately Tim reached out for my hand right then. He looked a little solemn, and I gave him a warm hug. As I began to walk away I heard him whisper to Ben, then Ben's quiet reply, "If she wanted our number, she would've asked."

Back on the road again I pressed on the accelerator, putting miles between me and the rest stop as quickly as possible, overcome with embarrassment. One look at Ben should've told me that this was a guy who had "trouble concentrating" on one girl. And surely one look at me must've told *him* that I didn't know how to act around guys. I started punching buttons, searching for a clear radio station, trying to put all thoughts of Ben behind me. Still my eyes darted after every faded red car on the highway. Do you know how many faded red cars drive the Jersey Turnpike?

Get real, I told myself. *And be glad you'll never see him again.*

The romantic holiday songs on the radio were getting to me. I pulled out a Jane's Addiction CD and shoved it into the player, then turned up the volume. Finding my exit, I rushed up the Garden State Parkway. Surely I'd left Ben and Tim miles behind, for there were a million exits to take from the Jersey Turnpike, and Ben and Tim could've been headed anywhere—Pennsylvania, Connecticut, Vermont, Canada. . . . Then I hit the brakes.

Had I really seen it—an old red Toyota stopped on the side of the road?

Two

*T*HERE COULDN'T BE *another Tomato Soup in the universe,* I thought as I pulled over to the shoulder, then backed up, my eyes on the beat-up little car in my rearview mirror. I noticed that it had a Blue Heron license plate, just like Miss Henny's; whoever owned the car lived in Maryland. No one was inside. I parked quickly and grabbed my car phone.

I'd barely gotten out of my Audi when Tim called to me. "Allie Cat! Over here!" He was waving his arms at me, standing about forty feet back in the roadside grass.

"Stay where you are, Tim. I told you to stay there," came a voice from under the car.

I walked around to the back of the Toyota. Ben's long legs were hanging out, the rest of him under the car.

"Hi . . . it's Allie. . . . Need help?"

"No. Just taking a coffee break," he grunted.

"Okay. I'm off."

"Allie!" he called, then slid himself out from beneath the car. He looked up at me and grinned. "Nice to see you again."

For a moment I couldn't think of what to say. I glanced down at my hands. "Yeah. Nice to see anyone with a car phone."

He sat up.

"Who do you want to call—Triple A?" I took several steps closer and held it out to him. If he touched my hand and looked in my eyes, would I tingle again or just get grease all over me?

"I think all I really need is a coat hanger," he said, wiping his hands on a towel. "All of ours are plastic. Do you have a wire one with you?"

"Yes," I said. "But I don't think it's going to hold those wheels on."

"It's for the muffler, Allie," he said, lying down again.

"Oh, you mean you have a muffler? It sure didn't sound like it when you left the rest stop."

He gave me a sarcastic smile, then pulled himself back under the Toyota.

"One wire coat hanger, coming up," I said cheerfully.

I fetched it for him, then stood around, watching his feet and listening to him grunt and mutter beneath the car. "What was that you said?" I teased. " 'Oh, fudge'?"

He kicked me, and I laughed.

"Is there something else I can do to help?" I asked after some more muttering from below.

"You can talk to Tim and keep him back from the road. That would be one less worry."

I went and sat in the grass with Tim. "I knew you'd come," he told me.

"How could you know that? You didn't know what road I was taking."

He shrugged and pulled on the coarse winter grass. "Things happen like that at Christmas," he said with a simple faith that touched me.

"Well, it was a lucky thing."

"Where are you going?" he asked.

"New York. My family lives on the other side of the Hudson River."

"Will you be there all of Christmas?" he asked.

"Yes."

"Maybe you could visit me."

"I'd like that, Tim," I answered. "But New York State is a big place and—"

"You have a car," he interrupted. "Do you know how to get to Thornhill?"

For a moment the town's name stuck in my throat. "Did you say Thornhill?"

"That's where my dad lives."

Maybe there was more than one Thornhill.

"It used to be where all of us lived. It's near Elmhurst—do you know where that is?"

I knew, all right. And I knew there was only one high school in the small town of Thornhill, the one in which my sisters had fast become the reigning queens. Ben and my sisters would probably know the same people, be part of the same cool crowd. What if he told a story about a silly girl named Allie who had tried flirting with him on the highway?

"Your cheeks get red a lot," Tim observed.

"It's cold out," I said, though I was warm inside. Despite my embarrassment, a tiny flame started to burn at the thought that I might see Ben again.

"It wasn't cold at the restaurant," Tim reminded me, "and they got red there too. Here comes Ben. He'll tell you how to get to Thornhill."

"He doesn't need to, Tim. That's where I'm going."

"You are? Yow!" He jumped up. "Hey, Ben." His brother was walking with long strides over the grass, looking satisfied with himself. "Guess where Allie's going?"

"In the other direction, hoping to lose us?" he joked.

"To Thornhill."

Ben stopped, though still a short distance from us. "You are?" His easy smile disappeared immediately. "Well . . . great," he said, walking the last few steps to us.

"My parents moved there in August," I told him. "I was only in town for two days, so I don't really know the place."

"There's not much to know." He sounded irritated—almost angry.

"All the friends I have live there," Tim told me wistfully.

16

"It's hard to be away from friends," I replied, turning to the little boy. "All mine are back at my boarding school."

"You'll do all right," Ben said curtly. "It's a small town."

I glanced up at him, mystified by the sudden coldness in his voice. What was his problem? Did he think that knowing no one else, I was going to follow him around like a puppy dog? Did he have such an ego that he thought a little flirting meant I was madly in love with him? Well, I'd set his mind at ease.

"Listen," I said, "I know you must have a ton of friends to see."

"I do," he replied without looking at me.

"All those girls who disturb your concentration," I continued.

He glanced sideways at me.

"But you don't have to worry about me adding to the distractions. I know it's tough. So many girls, so little time." I sighed, my voice oozing with false sympathy.

He stared at me.

"I'm off, guys. Maybe I'll run into you two weeks from now on the turnpike headed south."

Ben didn't reply until I had strode twenty feet away. "Did I say something wrong?" he asked.

"No." I gave them a half wave. "You didn't say anything at all." *Like, "I hope we can get together,"* I thought.

I roared off in my car. When I was a chance

meeting, some girl Ben thought he'd never see again, he was charming. But when he found out we were heading for the same town . . . *Well, he'll be sorry,* I told myself. *When he sees my gorgeous sisters, he'll be begging to visit my home.*

Not that that was any consolation.

"Sweetheart!" my mother greeted me when I walked in the kitchen an hour later. She had the portable phone cradled between her ear and shoulder, a glue gun in one hand and a tumble of wine-colored ribbon in the other. "I have to go, Linda," she said into the phone. "My firstborn is home."

"Mom, couldn't you just refer to me as Allie?" I asked as I took the phone from her shoulder and clicked it off. We hugged. I had become adept at hugging my mother with drapes and paintbrushes and wallpaper rolls in her hands. Every time my parents moved, she redecorated, and if they stayed in the same place for more than two years, she redid the interior just out of habit. "You look great, Mom."

"You too—only a little thin."

She'd been saying that since I was in sixth grade. Maybe she was still waiting for me to get the full, curvy figure she and my sisters had. The three of them had light hair and green eyes. But I was built just like my father and aunt Jen—tall and slim, and sharing their dark coloring as well.

"You're just in time. I have to decide which wreath looks best on the front door." She attached the bow she was holding to a wreath that lay on the long kitchen table next to five others. "I know I can use all of these somewhere."

"You can never have too many wreaths," I replied, smiling. When it comes to decorating, my mother can never have too many of anything—wallpaper patterns, flowered rugs, furniture with carved doodads. Which is why she fell in love with the Victorian town of Thornhill and its wooden nineteenth-century houses painted in a rainbow of colors.

"Can you help carry these?" my mother asked.

I looped one wreath around my neck like a tire and carried two on each arm, keeping my arms outstretched as I followed her out the back door and around to the front. Just as I got to the front steps a BMW pulled into our driveway, its old motor revved too high. The guy driving it saw me and turned to my sisters with a questioning look on his face.

Sandra climbed out from the backseat. "Hey," she called out, "it's a walking Christmas tree."

"Allie, you're home!" Julia said as she got out of the car. "Thanks, Ford." She gave a vague wave as the guy backed his car down the driveway. While I'm a novice at flirting, I'm an expert at reading my sisters. Julia's wave told me Ford was either a new candidate or a boyfriend fading fast—there was no commitment in that wave.

"You look terrific, Al," Julia teased. "But I think you need a little more tinsel on top."

"No, dear, that's my subtle wreath," Mom explained, fingering the decoration that hung around my neck. It was silver, covered with metallic birds dipped in blue and pink glitter.

"Real subtle, Mom," Sandra said, running her hand through blond hair that fell to her waist. Julia's did too, but she usually wore hers up in some way. Sandra smiled at me. "I'm glad to see you, Al."

"Thanks."

"Me too," Julia added. "We missed our big sister. We especially missed you when we had to write papers."

"Everybody at Fields has been asking about you," I told them. "I've got a million messages and cards for you."

"Really?" Julia said, but she didn't sound very interested.

"Miss Henny wanted me to say hello for her."

"That's nice. So which of these wreaths is going on the front door?" Sandra asked Mom.

"That's what I'm trying to decide," she replied.

"Miss Henny's talking about retiring soon," I went on, "and—"

"She should've five years ago," Sandra remarked.

"Come on, Allie," Julia said, "go stand by the door. Model the wreaths for us."

Apparently they were no longer interested in people at Fields. I gave up and dutifully climbed the steps of the porch. My mother and sisters stood a distance back, studying the decorations, directing me to hold each one up at various heights. I did this for three rounds while they argued over which looked best, then I finally got fed up and lined up the wreaths by the door.

"I'm unpacking," I said, heading toward my car, which was parked at the end of the driveway, back near the kitchen.

"I'll help you," Julia volunteered. "How was the drive up?" she asked, trailing behind me.

"Okay." I popped open the trunk. Julia pulled out a basketball and started dribbling to the backboard mounted on the double garage.

"Good shot, Jule!" I called as the ball swished through the net.

She dribbled back to me, then pulled out a lacrosse stick and two tennis rackets. "I'll put these in the exercise room," she said, heading toward the back door.

Sandra circled the porch and joined me. "The wreath with the glittery birds won."

"I thought it would."

She gazed down into the trunk. "Wow—you packed light."

Sandra never went anywhere without several suitcases of clothes. I handed her two bags of gifts, then followed her into the house, carrying my one suitcase and a box of videos. We went through the kitchen and into the hall, then climbed the wide, turning stair in the center of the house.

Sandra stopped abruptly at the entrance to my room. "Oops."

"Oops?" I repeated, trying to see over her shoulder.

"Guess we should leave your stuff right here. *Julia!*" she bellowed.

It took the three of us twenty minutes to clear their things out of my room. Why my sisters needed to drape their stuff over my bed and chairs, I don't know, because all three of our rooms were big. Sandra's and mine faced the front of the house, and we both had a bay window with a window seat. Sandra had a private bathroom as well. Julia, whose room was in the back of the house, shared a bathroom with me when I was home, but her room had a door to an outside deck. Our parents have always been careful to balance what they give to each of us. Since I'm away at school, I got to keep our car, but it's understood that when I'm home, my sisters can borrow it and I'm expected to do errands.

With their stuff put away, I opened my suitcase on the double bed. My sisters stretched out on either side of it.

"You don't still wear this?" Sandra said, pulling out a raspberry-colored sweater.

"It's my favorite."

"It was your favorite two years ago," she observed.

"So, I'm loyal." I took it out of her hands and put it in a drawer.

Julia was holding a small blue bag. "Where's your makeup case?"

"That's it," I replied.

"It has one lipstick and a tube of sunscreen."

"That's it," I repeated.

Julia sat up and put on the dark lipstick. It did nothing for her gilt-and-porcelain look.

"Wipe it off," Sandra advised.

"Did you get any good Christmas gifts at school?" Julia asked.

"Some things, but I left them in my dorm room."

"Anything from a guy?" Sandra wanted to know.

An image of Ben's face suddenly flashed in my mind. I quickly forced it away. "Why? Are those the only gifts that count?"

"I was just curious," Sandra replied. "Don't be so sensitive, Al." She played with the beaded bracelet on her left arm.

"That's pretty," I said, hoping to ward off any further interest in my social life.

"Mike gave it to me."

"Mike . . ." I couldn't remember who he was. My sisters and I e-mailed each other about once a week, but I lost track of all their guys.

"Mike Calloway, jock and heartthrob," Julia filled me in. "Basketball hero of Thornhill High. Very, very cute. Very, very stuck on Sandra."

"A basketball player," I said. "You can wear four-inch heels!"

Sandra threw back her head and laughed. "I've bought three pairs this month. But he's not a boyfriend, not yet, and I'm not sure he's so stuck on me." She rolled off the bed and got up to look at herself in the mirror. "Sometimes I think he's more hooked on his sport."

"Well, if you didn't play so hard to get," Julia chastised her. She turned to me. "You've never seen such games—one moment they chase each other down the halls, the next moment they're ignoring each other."

Sandra shrugged—a pretty, sulky shrug.

"How about you, Julia?" I asked, continuing to put things away. "Who was the guy who dropped you off?"

"Ford?" She gave a shrug almost identical to Sandra's, then sighed. Having already noted the vague wave, I figured he was Boyfriend Past.

"He and I starred in *Broadway Revue,* the fall production at school."

"And?" I prompted.

"He's great looking."

"I *saw.*"

"He's got a good voice," Julia continued. "And a lot of ideas for fun things to do."

"But?"

"It's not true love." She picked up a pillow, held it in her arms like a person, then gave it a poke. "Unfortunately he was more interesting when he was playing a role."

"Maybe he's just having a hard time being himself," I suggested, "you know, letting you see who he really is."

"You think so?"

"I don't know what you're bummed about," Sandra said to Julia. "Two other guys called you last night."

"Three," Julia corrected Sandra sweetly.

"No, Jeff's call was for me. He had us mixed up."

"I don't think so."

The identical stiff smiles and perfect enunciation of each word warned me that one of the twins' competitive matches was coming on. I'd witnessed enough of them for a lifetime and decided my sisters could battle it out somewhere else. "Listen," I said, "I need to hide your Christmas gifts."

"Okay, we'll close our eyes," Julia replied with a sly smile.

"Out!" I told them.

Sandra laughed.

"Come down for a snack when you're done," Julia said.

As soon as my sisters were gone I put the shopping bags in the closet—where, if the twins wanted, they could easily find their gifts—but hid the three romances I'd brought home to read. My recent switch from Stephen King to gothic love stories was something I preferred to keep to myself.

It took longer than it should have to put everything away because I kept pausing to think about Ben—his smile, the warmth of his voice, his sense of humor. And the way it all shut down when he learned he might see me again.

It wasn't fair! My sisters had an army of guys to choose from while I just wanted to be with one—and he just wanted to be with me . . . when no other girl was around.

Three

BY THE TIME I finished unpacking, two of my sisters' friends had dropped by. My mother, always trying to help along my social life, had been holding back the snacks and sodas, waiting for me to come down. When she asked me to carry them into the family room, I knew she was hoping I'd stay and talk to my sisters' friends. The fact that I was vice president of the senior class and captain of the basketball and softball teams at Fields didn't re-assure her; I had to have friends at home too.

When I walked in the room, my sisters intro-duced me to Caroline, who had a mane of red hair, and Janice, who had silky black hair and incredible almond-shaped eyes. I placed the tray in the center of the group, aware of the two girls studying me.

"Stay," Julia said, catching me by the hand as I turned to walk out. "It's Christmas vacation. Party down, Al."

Before I could reply, Janice said, "So you go to boarding school."

"Yes," I answered, then took a tentative step toward the door.

"An all-girl school," she continued, her dark eyes full of curiosity.

I felt like a strange species she'd just discovered. "The same one my sisters went to," I told her.

Julia yanked on my hand, pulling me down into their circle. I sat on the floor, figuring I could leave as soon as the questions were over.

"I can't even imagine what that is like!" Janice exclaimed.

"I told you what it's like," Julia reminded her.

But Janice shook her head. "Mostly you told me about the guys at the boarding school three miles away."

Everyone laughed.

"Three miles, is it?" Caroline mused, munching on some of the chips I'd brought in. "Well, that's a mile and a half for the girl and a mile and a half for the guy. Do you ever have secret late night meetings in the woods?"

"Uh, no," I responded.

"For that kind of meeting you'd have to get across a river and up a steep hill, almost a cliff," Julia said.

"I tried it once with David Crane," Sandra added, "but he got lost. How is David?" she asked me.

"I don't know." I reached for a pretzel. "I haven't seen him since last year."

"You're kidding!" Sandra sounded genuinely surprised. "But you two liked to talk. You always kept him company for me down in the waiting parlor. At Fields," she explained to her friends, "when the guys came to pick us up, they had to sign in and stay in the waiting parlor."

And guess who used to be sent down to keep all those guys company? While Sandra would finish dressing, David and I would discuss an entire week of sports.

"You know," Sandra said, "I thought with me gone, he'd be sure to date you."

I gritted my teeth. "Guess not."

"Are you an actress too?" Janice asked me, her dark hair swinging forward.

"Janice is going to be the director of our spring production," Julia told me. "She is so, *so* talented."

"Oh, you drama club types," Caroline said, laughing at them. "The way you suck up to each other, telling each other you're wonderful."

"But I *am* wonderful," Janice teased, stretching back into the luxury of a leather chair.

Julia playfully poked Caroline. "At least we're fans of each other and not just the guys' team."

"Caroline is captain of the cheerleading squad," Sandra explained.

"But Sandra *should* be," Caroline told me. "She cheers louder than any member of my squad when Mike takes the floor. What a defection! Our number-one jock interested in someone from the drama club rather than the cheerleading squad."

29

"But that's not so different from last year," Janice argued from her chair. "Do you remember Ben Harrington?"

My ears pricked up.

"What girl could forget Ben?" Caroline replied.

My Ben?

Caroline combed her fingers through her long, fiery hair. "Now *he* was hot. Too bad he had to leave. His parents got divorced—my mother says Ben's mother was dumped for another woman. He and his little brother moved away," she went on, "to Maryland, I think."

I sat up so straight that Janice glanced at me.

"I wonder if Ben is related to Aunt Jen's friend," Sandra said to Julia. "Isn't his name Harrington?"

"I heard Ben's coming back for the holidays," Caroline continued. "I hope he's driving something better than that red Toyota."

I barely breathed.

"He must've dated every girl on the cheerleading squad," she said, "and in the drama club. The sailing club too—the blondes, usually."

And *I* had tried to flirt with him? My earlier suspicion was right—Ben must've known from the beginning that I didn't know how to flirt and had simply found me entertaining. The final brush-off made more sense than ever.

"The thing about Ben," Janice said, "is that he's truly a nice person. He always had as many guy friends as girls. I guess because he knew he was cool, he could be nice to everyone—people

I wouldn't be caught dead talking to."

Like me, I thought.

"I'm counting on you to introduce us," Sandra said.

"Yeah, well, you're going to have to stand in line," Caroline told her.

"And do it when Mike's not around," Janice advised. "Mike was never as popular as Ben, and it really bothered him. He won't want you hanging around him."

"No guy tells me who I can be friends with," Sandra retorted.

"I could sure use a break from Ford," Julia added.

Déjà vu. I'd seen it all before—my sisters quickly moving in on the most interesting guy around, deflating everyone else's hopes. The thing was, until now it hadn't been *my* secret hope that was squashed. It was a very tiny hope, of course, one I hadn't wanted to admit to myself. But now I knew better. Me and the hottest guy in town? When the moon dropped out of the sky, maybe.

My sisters and their friends went on to discuss other guys and girls in their crowd—who was in and who was out. The names meant nothing to me, though occasionally Ben's name would surface. I found myself wondering if there was a pretty girl at Thornhill High whom he hadn't dated.

It was a relief when I spotted my father standing in the doorway, listening to our conversation, looking perplexed. Sometimes my dad seems like a lost

31

soul in his own household. The others turned and saw him.

"Ladies," he said, nodding at us. He always gets formal when he's uncomfortable.

"Hey, Dad."

"Allison," he said. "Welcome home! May I take you away from your friends for a moment?"

My friends? I got up quickly and followed him through the living room into his study. It was the one room that always felt familiar to me, for the books, furniture, and my father's sculpture collection had followed us from house to house.

"Well, Allie, you look—you look—" Sometimes my father thought too much about his words.

"Like Allie?" I suggested.

He smiled and gave me a quick hug, then retreated behind his wide desk.

"So how's it going, Dad?" I asked, sitting down across from him.

"The Dow fell last quarter, but I'm confident that it'll turn around once stockholders recognize the importance of our new investments in Malaysia. The drilling is almost completed, and the mine samples are positive. It's a matter of getting the right supervisory personnel."

That's my father for you, cuts right to the chase. He's totally uncomfortable with small talk and would've given me the same answer if I'd asked, "How are *you*, Dad?" He is how his work is.

"How about you?" he inquired.

"Well, I sent out the college applications."

"And?"

"I included Harvard and Princeton. I mean, why not shoot for the best? I can deal with rejection."

"That's my girl," he said, looking proud. "Jen called this morning," he added.

"About tonight? She e-mailed me last week, asking if I could have dinner with her."

"Yes, well, there's been a slight change of plans. The dinner is still on, but you'll be meeting later than she'd planned at a restaurant called Candella's."

"Great," I said. "What time?"

"Eight. Aunt Jen has a surprise for you."

"Yeah?"

He nodded. "Quite a surprise."

I got the feeling he didn't fully approve of it, but that wasn't unusual. Jen is my father's youngest sister, an independent type who will go anywhere and try anything. She's single, thirty, and has a very successful law practice in Elmhurst. She's my godmother and with my parents living abroad has been a confidante to me. For the last three years we'd talked about taking a month-long trip to celebrate my graduation from high school. I hoped that was what this dinner was about.

"Candella's is an upscale place, but your mother can fill you in on that," he said, which was the signal that our talk was over.

"Thanks, Dad."

"Thanks, Allison," he said when I was almost at the doorway, "for coming home."

Four

M Y SISTERS SHOWED up in my room the moment I began to dress for Candella's. The result was a spread of cosmetics like that in a department store offering free makeovers. I made the mistake of saying that I didn't know what to do with half the bottles and brushes. The twins went right to work on me, talking all the time.

"Find out if Aunt Jen's boyfriend, Sam Harrington, is related to Ben," Sandra told me, squinting at the line she'd just drawn on my eyelid.

"Is she actually dating Mr. Harrington?" I asked. Jen hadn't mentioned him to me. Each of us had our special aunt, and Jen, being mine, usually told me something important before she told my sisters.

"As much as Aunt Jen dates anyone," Julia answered.

"He's old," Sandra told me. "Too old."

"He's got gray hair," Julia added.

"There!" Sandra said, looking satisfied. Then

35

she caught my face with a light hand. "Don't look yet. Some lips, huh?" she asked Julia.

Julia nodded. "I'm glad you're finally letting us fix you up, Allie. What changed your mind?"

I shrugged. I wasn't sure why I decided to let them make me up that evening or borrow the dress Julia pulled out of her closet with the excuse that it was the wrong color for her. It was the shortest, sexiest piece of velveteen I'd ever put on. Maybe I was making an effort to find some connection with my sisters, or maybe I wanted to feel less like a boarding-school bumpkin who had embarrassed herself flirting with Thornhill's biggest hunk. A half hour later I stared at the dark-haired girl in the mirror and thought that Miss Henny might've been right—I did have my "own beauty."

"Good lord!" my father exclaimed when I passed him in the hall.

"You look beautiful, Allie, just beautiful," my mother said.

"You think I should bring my driver's license so Aunt Jen knows it's me?"

"Chin up. Walk straight," my mother replied, "and don't talk that way."

As I drove the short route to Candella's a new kind of excitement grew in me. I felt glamorous, adventurous. I handed my coat to the guy in the cloakroom and didn't hunch over like a schoolgirl when he checked me out before checking the coat. Aunt Jen came in right behind me. We hugged.

"You look wonderful!" she exclaimed.

I'd never seen her cheeks so pink. "So do you."

She deposited her beaver jacket, then grabbed my hand. "This wasn't what I'd planned for us tonight, but come on," she said, "our table's waiting."

I strutted after my aunt and the maitre d' with an amazing burst of confidence. Maybe it was the attention my family had lavished on me that afternoon or the cute guy at the corner table who turned to look at me and smiled, but for one unusual moment I was feeling so adult and sure of myself, I was ready for anything.

But I never could have been prepared for what happened next. Because one second later I noticed Ben and Tim Harrington across the room—right in the direction where we were headed. Just as I was about to suggest to Aunt Jen that we go somewhere else so I could bolt out of there as quickly as possible, Tim looked up and saw me.

"Hey!" he called. "It's Allie Cat!"

Ben looked up with surprise. His eyes flicked quickly to Aunt Jen, then he turned to the grayhaired man with whom he was sitting. Ben, Tim, and the man, who must have been their father, rose at the same time as Jen and I walked toward them.

Were we sitting with *them?* My legs suddenly felt wobbly. "Hey, Tim," I said softly.

My aunt looked back at me. "You know each other?"

Tim turned to Ben, who was staring at me as if he had just been pinged between the eyes with a rock. Tim nudged him. "It's Allie."

The older man held out his hand to me. "I'm Sam Harrington," he introduced himself in a deep and friendly voice. "You don't by any chance drive a silver Audi and make highway rescues?"

"Uh . . . sometimes."

"Will somebody explain this to me?" Aunt Jen said. "I'm the one who was supposed to be springing a surprise." She playfully flashed a bright, sparkly object on her left hand.

"What's that?" I asked.

Aunt Jen smiled. "I'm getting married, Allie."

I guess I gave her the same shot-between-the-eyes look as Ben had given me.

"Allie?" my aunt asked, leaning closer to me.

"Wonderful," I sputtered out. "Congratulations. That's great. Really."

Not really. My adventurous aunt was settling down. The person in my family whom I most wanted to be like was "the other woman" in a divorce—the woman Ben had told me he wanted nothing to do with. And the guy I'd flirted with because I thought I'd never see him again was going to be connected to me by marriage.

"Why don't we all sit down?" Mr. Harrington suggested.

There was a moment of confusion as Tim crawled under the table so he could take the seat next to me. We seated ourselves around the circle, Tim and Ben on either side of me. At least I didn't have to look squarely at Ben. Instead I studied the strong shape of his left hand and kept smelling his aftershave.

"You look pretty."

I turned to my ardent admirer, Tim. "Thanks. That's a nice sweater."

"*She* gave it to me," he said, with a quick glance toward my aunt.

"Her name is Jen," his father said sternly.

"You already told me," Tim replied. "Twice."

This, I thought, *is not going to be a fun dinner.*

"Tim, did you know Jen is Allie's aunt?" Mr. Harrington asked.

Tim looked at me as if I'd just betrayed him.

"So, Allie," Mr. Harrington said, pulling on his tie, which did not go with his shirt, which did not go with his jacket, "Jen tells me that you attend Fields and you're a top-notch student and excellent athlete."

I stared back at him for a moment, still trying to absorb the fact that this man—Ben's *father* of all people—was going to marry Aunt Jen. I hadn't even known she was dating anyone! Then I remembered that a question had been directed at me. "Yes. I mean, I like school, and I play sports."

"Terrific. So does Ben," Mr. Harrington said.

"Really, you two share a lot of interests," Aunt Jen added.

Just what Ben wants to hear, I thought. I figured his palms were getting clammy at the idea that he might be asked to entertain me over the holidays. *Well, let him sweat. Let him worry that I'm going to join the army of girls who dream of having something in common with him.*

"Ben used to be a basketball player," Tim volunteered. "And lacrosse. And soccer. He was the best and used to get his picture in our paper all the time, and when he was a sophomore, he won All-State Center, and when he was a junior, he won—"

"Tim," Ben said, "give it a rest. She's not interested in all that."

"How do you know?" I asked.

"It's boring," Ben replied. "And it's no longer relevant."

"Maybe it's just boring to you because you already know it all," I pointed out.

"All right," he said stiffly, "we have about ten scrapbooks at home you can go through."

"One will be enough."

He turned and met my gaze steadily.

"Then I'll show you mine," I said.

I heard Mr. Harrington stifle a laugh. He reached for my aunt's hand. "You're right, Jen. She's just like you."

Once again I couldn't help staring at Mr. Harrington. This was going to take some time to get used to.

"Can I see your book too?" Tim asked me.

"Oh, Tim, I was just kidding. I don't really keep things like that."

"When I was in high school," Mr. Harrington said, "the girls always kept dance invitations, party streamers, things like that. A guy knew he'd made a good impression on a date when the girl asked to keep the ticket stub."

"Do you have scrapbooks with stuff like that?" Tim asked me.

When I didn't answer, Ben replied, "Ten of them. Maybe she'll show you one."

I turned quickly. "According to the girls who live here—some of my sisters' friends—ten memory books are *far* less than you've helped to fill."

There was a moment of silence in which I told myself I hadn't said that aloud. But Ben's raised eyebrows told me I had.

"Really," he said, in a tone I couldn't interpret.

"Are you ready to order?" our server asked, arriving at our table just in time. Maybe I should have requested my own bread basket so I could stuff my mouth before I said anything else I'd regret. Now Ben would think I'd been doing research on him.

"Your sisters are the twins," Mr. Harrington said after we had all placed our orders, "the ones who made such a sensation in the school drama production this fall, is that right?"

"Yes, sir."

"Please," he said, "call me Sam."

"Sam," I repeated.

"We carried a story about the Parker twins in our newspaper," Sam told Ben. "Craig took the photos for us."

"Well, Craig always does a good job," Ben replied. His voice held no enthusiasm for the conversation, and I noticed that he wouldn't look at my aunt Jen. I felt bad for her even if she was "the other woman."

41

"I remember now," I said. "Mom mailed me the article."

"Sam is the publisher of the paper," Aunt Jen told me. I could hear the pride in her voice.

"Yeah? That's cool."

Sam grinned. "That's how we met, you know. I interviewed Jen."

Bad move. I saw Ben's hand tense up.

"I thought she was the brightest and prettiest woman I'd ever had coffee with."

I saw Aunt Jen shake her head at Sam. *Shut up,* I silently urged him.

"And tough," he added. "When I asked her for a follow-up interview, she refused. She made me ask her three times."

I knew someone had to change the subject. "I can't wait till you meet my sisters," I said. "You'll really like them."

"Do they look like you?" Tim asked. "Then you'd be triplets." He laughed at his own joke.

I laughed with him. "No, you'd never guess we're sisters. They're gorgeous."

Out of the corner of my eye I saw Ben frowning.

"I need to make a phone call," Aunt Jen said. "Would you come with me, Sam?"

I knew Sam was going to get a lecture on what to say in front of the kids. The last thing his sons wanted to hear was how he fell in love with someone other than their mother.

When Jen disappeared with Tim's father, the little boy asked, "How come your sisters live here and you don't? Did your parents get a divorce?"

"No, it's just that my sisters like to party and date a lot and wanted to go to a regular high school, like the one here."

I caught Ben studying me, almost as if he were sizing up me and my family. "My sisters have always been the most popular girls at school, first at Fields, and now at Thornhill," I boasted, then immediately felt stupid. What did that have to do with anything? But when Ben looked unimpressed, as if he already knew a million girls like my sisters, I became defiant. "Guys can't resist them. You'll see."

"These are the sisters whose friends filled you in on my past?" he asked.

"Yes. Apparently you're a hot topic of conversation at Thornhill High," I told him. "Trust me," I added quickly, "I didn't bring you up."

One side of Ben's mouth pulled up in a mocking smile. Was he laughing at me or the other girls? I wondered. He sure didn't look happy. Nor did Tim, who had begun folding his napkin over and over into the same shape, his chin down low on his chest.

The anger began to drain out of me. There was enough hurt with the divorce and remarriage situation; I didn't need to add to it by saying snide things to Ben. One of us had to make things pleasant—otherwise we'd never get through this dinner or the holidays.

"Tim, did you just see those cakes go by?" I asked, pointing to a cart.

The little boy nodded.

"Go find out what's on there, see what we can have for dessert, okay?"

"You getting rid of me?" Tim asked.

"Yup."

His eyes crinkled up with his smile. He rose and followed the waiter across the room.

"Look," I said, turning to Ben, "we need to straighten out a few things."

"Like what?"

"Well, let's start at the beginning. Back at the rest stop, I kind of flirted."

"Not kind of," he observed.

"It was . . . sort of an experiment. At an all–girls school we don't get much chance to practice, so—"

"I see. I was your guinea pig."

"The good news is that you don't have to worry about me chasing you around."

"I know—you told me that back on the Garden State."

"Moving on," I continued, "I shouldn't have mentioned my sisters or—"

"Why not?" he replied quickly. "I love to know that people are gossiping about me."

"Help me out here," I warned him between tight lips. "You're making me mad."

"Sorry . . . sorry," he repeated, sounding sincere the second time.

I took a deep breath. "I understand that you're not thrilled to meet my family and that you wouldn't like anyone related to Aunt Jen. I'd feel the same way if I were you."

He played with his fork, turning it over and over in his hands.

"But I think we should try to make this one meal a friendly one," I told him, "for other people's sake."

"Do you mean for the sake of my father and his fiancée? I don't care how they feel."

"How about Tim?" I asked.

Ben dropped the fork, then sat back in his chair. "You've got a soft spot for him, don't you?"

"Guess so."

"I think you'll go down in *Tim's* scrapbook as his first love."

I blushed. Ben glanced sideways at me, a trace of a smile on his lips.

"Okay," he said, his face growing serious again. "I know you're right. But I'm telling you, I'm in a stinking mood. At the moment I'd like to kill my father, and I don't even want to think about your aunt Jen. So you're gonna have to be ready to change the wrong topics of conversation my father is so adept at introducing and stomp on my foot if I start acting up."

"No problem," I replied. "I'm wearing my sister's spikes."

His mouth softened again, and his eyes got the teasing look I'd seen back on the turnpike. "No, you're not," he said, rubbing the toe of his shoe under the arch of my stockinged foot. "You took them off the moment you sat down."

Five

TUESDAY MORNING WOULD have been dismal in any month other than December. But when I awoke, three hours later than usual, the gray, sleety mix falling outside was warmed by Christmas lights inside. My mother must have tiptoed in and lit the candles in my bedroom windows. In the hall the pine garland that was wrapped around the railing of the second-floor balcony twinkled its way down the steps, leading me from landing to landing. I found my mother in the kitchen, working with her faithful glue gun.

"We're going to have to get you a holster for that," I said, coming up behind her. "G'morning, Mom."

"Morning, sweetheart."

I poured myself some juice and sat down at the table across from where she was attaching little gold horns to some kind of white twig arrangement. "Where are you going to put that?" I asked.

"These are for New Year's, sweetie. We'll be taking them as gifts when we make Christmas visits. For the first time since you girls were tiny, we're just a town away from relatives, at least on your father's and Jen's side."

"How long have you known about Aunt Jen and Sam?" I asked.

"Jen told us this past weekend. I don't think your father is real happy about it, given that Sam is recently divorced, and, well, he is a little eccentric." My mother fussed with the wreath, twisting its leaves. "Anyway, she wanted to tell you in person, and we let your sisters know last night when you were out. Speaking of which—"

"Yes?"

"Could you pick them up from school? It's their last day and early dismissal. I told them to look for you."

"No problem."

"The roads may be icy, and I trust you more than their boyfriends," my mother went on. "Not that they aren't nice boys, every one of them. Now, the one that—"

"I understand, Mom. I'm glad to do it," I said, cutting her off before she went page by page through the current boyfriend catalog.

A few hours later, when I pulled on my old parka, which showed the wear of many camping expeditions, another reason for my mission was revealed.

"You're wearing that?" my mother asked with a frown.

"It's cold out."

"Here," she said, producing a coat so quickly, either she'd learned magic or had fetched it earlier from Sandra's closet. It was made of soft white rain-repellent fabric and had a fur-edged hood that could make Sandra look like Julie Christie in the old movie *Dr. Zhivago.*

"It's not mine, Mom."

"Wear it," she said, pointing her glue gun at me. "And enjoy yourself," she added in a more motherly voice. "Meet some nice boys."

She never gives up, I thought, stuffing the map she'd drawn for me in my pocket.

When I arrived at the school, the lot was filled with cars. I was a few minutes early and feeling restless, so I parked my car and got out to walk. The icy rain had stopped, and a blustery wind was beginning to blow. I was glad I had the hood to pull up over my head.

I strolled along the pavement in front of the school until I reached a long, rectangular wing of the building with a rounded top—the gym, I figured. Suddenly a door opened and Ben emerged. He was wearing a dark gold jacket, the kind a member of a school team wears. His eyes were far away, and his lips held a straight, almost grim line. I took a step back, unsure of whether to speak to him. If he saw me as I turned my back, he might think I was snubbing him. But he didn't look as if he wanted to talk to anyone either.

I turned to retrace my steps and accidentally

kicked a loose stone. He turned his head quickly.

"Hi," I said.

"Hi."

"How are you?" I asked.

"Okay."

"Good."

There was an awkward silence. Ben glanced at his watch.

"I'm here to pick up my sisters," I explained quickly. "It just happens that I keep ending up in the same place as you. My mother sent me."

He laughed. "It's okay, Allie. I know you're not chasing me."

I nodded and turned to continue my walk alone, but Ben fell in stride beside me.

"Were you visiting old friends?" I asked when it was clear he was strolling with me rather than trying to get somewhere.

"I just saw one of my teachers and my coach, Tweeter."

"Tweeter?"

"That's his nickname."

"I bet he was glad to see you," I said.

"How would you know?"

I blinked.

"Sorry," Ben apologized, "I'm still in that stinking mood. Though I faked pretty well last night, don't you think?"

"You did great. Tim actually called Jen by her own name once. Still, faking is hard to keep up for too long."

"Sometimes there isn't any choice," he murmured.

"How's Tomato Soup doing?" I asked, switching to a lighter subject.

"She's being good, hoping Santa will bring her a new engine."

I laughed and so did he, but I could hear the effort behind his laugh. "No one's around," I told him as we walked. "It's all right to be in a stinking mood till your friends come out."

He turned and gazed down at me. For one crazy moment I felt as beautiful as Julie Christie in that fur-lined hood.

"It'll get better," I promised him. "You're back with your old friends now, kids who know you."

Ben looked away.

"I'm sorry it's so hard for you."

"It's much harder on Tim," he replied. "He doesn't understand why any of this happened. I have to keep telling him it has nothing to do with him or me—we didn't make our parents unhappy. But I'm not sure I'm getting through. Our lunch at the rest stop was the first time I'd seen him laugh for a long while."

"If it'll help," I said, "I'll be glad to take him out during the vacation—to a movie or skating, whatever. He'll be a good distraction. Really," I added in response to Ben's curious look, "it's going to be a long two weeks for me. I'd enjoy doing things with Tim."

We had reached the end of the lot and turned back, walking silently for a minute.

"Why is it going to be a long two weeks?"

"Just is."

A gust of wind blew back my hood. I could feel my hair turning into a million feathers and put my hand up as if I could hold them down.

He studied my face. "Because you left behind a boyfriend?"

The school bell rang, saving me from laughing at his guess. I turned with relief as the school doors banged back.

"Benjo!" someone called. Three guys wearing the same gold jacket as Ben came hurrying toward us.

"Harrington! Where have you been, man?" the tallest said.

"Hey, Twist!" Ben replied. They did some macho body banging, one of those things about guys I'll never understand.

"It's Ben!" said a girl who'd just emerged from the school building.

"Hi, Ben," two others called.

"He's ba–ack," teased the tall guy named Twist.

A dozen people headed in our direction. I began to back away as they surrounded him.

"Ben, you look so good!" cooed a brunette.

"How come you didn't come back for home-coming?" another girl asked.

"Yeah, Lenny came back."

"I know," Ben replied, "I've talked to Lenny a couple of times this fall."

"You didn't talk to me, big guy," Twist said. He had a long and comical face to go with his long body. "I'm hurt."

Ben laughed.

They were all around him now. I looked for my sisters and their two friends I'd met the day before, but they hadn't come out yet. From my place at the edge of the crowd I could see that Ben's popularity with the girls hadn't been exaggerated. He was getting a lot of hugs and kisses. A girl with white blond hair and blue eyes attached herself to Ben's side as if they'd been glue-gunned together by my mother.

"What plans do you have for the holidays?" asked one of the guys in a gold jacket.

"Plans? None at the moment."

"To party, party, party," another guy said. "Your name's Ben Harrington, isn't it?"

Ben laughed. There wasn't a trace of the guy with the distant eyes and grim mouth.

"And you *do* have plans tonight," said the white blonde. "You're coming with me to Melanie's party."

"Melanie is having her usual?" Ben asked.

"Of course."

Fifteen people started talking at once, then I heard Ben say, "I just remembered. I can't. I promised Tim I'd take him to the holiday show at his old school."

"You've got to come," Twist urged.

"Someone else can take your brother," the light-haired girl said.

"I'll take him," I said.

Everyone turned around to see who had spoken.

"I told you, Ben, I'd be happy to do things with Tim."

Ben smiled, but I felt as if everyone else was

measuring me and my numbers didn't qualify. A few heads leaned toward each other; girls whispered. *They're curious, not snotty,* I told myself. *They're only looking to see who I am.* But their stares made me self-conscious.

"What if we both take Tim to the show," Ben suggested, "then go late to the party?"

"The problem is," said the girl with the light hair, "it's not my party. I can take a date, but I can't invite others."

"Are you sure?" Twist asked.

"Yeah. It's a closed party," said another girl.

Ben's eyes flicked from them to me. He looked a little embarrassed.

I just wanted to get out of there. "It's no big deal," I said. "I'm not in the mood for partying anyway. Really." I pulled my mother's map out of my pocket. "Write down your address and the time I should be there."

He seemed uncertain.

"Don't be pigheaded."

"Who, me?" Ben replied with a smile. "Okay. Thanks, Allie. You're a pal."

As soon as he'd scribbled down the information I took the map and headed toward the car to wait for my sisters. I pulled up my hood so Ben's friends couldn't see any part of my face. Didn't they know it was rude to stare? And as for their closed party, did I say I wanted to come?

I hadn't gotten far when I heard quick footsteps behind me. Someone caught me by the arm. "Hey, babe," he said. "Come on, slow down," he chided me, catching me lightly by the other arm. "Don't play games."

That was the last straw. I whirled around. I must've had one fierce expression on my face, for the guy stepped back quickly, holding his hands up in front of him. His dark blue eyes traveled down my coat and back up to my face. He was several inches taller than I and athletically built, his hair dark and wavy. "Who are you?" he asked.

"Who am I?" I snarled. "Who are *you*, Cupcake?"

The crowd behind him snickered. Ben laughed out loud. My sisters, who'd finally emerged from the school building, smiled and waved to me—or maybe to the studly guy staring at me.

"Mike," Sandra called out. "That's my sister Allie. She's just wearing my coat."

"Your sister," Mike echoed.

"Sorry," I apologized, "I didn't realize—"

"That's okay. My mistake," he said, continuing to gaze at me with an intensity that made me uncomfortable.

"I know, I know, I look nothing like my sisters."

"That's *very* okay," he said.

"So . . . uh . . . you're Sandra's friend."

"I'm friends with a lot of people," he replied, smiling at me.

"Well, it was nice meeting you," I told him, and extended my hand. He held it gently; I shook his hard, then walked away.

Mike joined Ben's crowd—my sisters' crowd. I

waited in the safety of my car while they all laughed and talked. I didn't want to look like I was watching, but I was dying to, especially as my sisters got closer to Ben. I busied myself by reading a state map of New York but still snuck peeks at them. Sandra was next to Ben, laughing, her golden hair flying loose in the breeze. I turned the map over and explored New Jersey. At last I heard the car door open.

"Thanks for waiting, Al," Julia said, climbing into the front seat.

"No problem," I replied.

"Is Ben ever cute!" Sandra exclaimed, throwing her books into the back of the car, then getting in. "Those big brown eyes. When he looks at you, you feel like he's kissing you."

I glanced at her in the rearview mirror, wishing for a short moment that her golden hair was mine. Then I pulled out of the parking space.

"I wonder . . . ," she said, her voice trailing off, her eyes getting dreamy.

"This is Sandra's latest thing," Julia told me. "She looks at a guy and predicts what it would be like to make out with him."

"How creative," I replied, and tried not to indulge myself in the same fantasy. "Buckle your seat belt."

"Oh!" Sandra cried. I'd taken the speed bump way too fast.

"Tell me," I said as I turned onto the street, "does the prediction ever get tested?"

Sandra smiled and settled back against the seat.

"Sooner or later," Julia responded.

Six

The harringtons' house wasn't far from ours, on a tree-lined avenue just off Hudson Street. When I arrived that evening, Tim answered the door, dancing with excitement. His father, dressed in faded jeans and a jacket with a Grateful Dead insignia, was ready to head back to the news-paper office. Sam was trying to make a deadline for the Christmas edition and had called earlier to ask if I could stay with Tim after the show. Now he thanked me several times, saying that Ben, who was already out, appreciated it too.

"I love Christmas shows," I told him, making sure Tim heard. I didn't want the kid to think he was an inconvenience being passed from person to person.

Actually, the show was fabulous entertainment. Several Christmas fairies forgot their lines, then started quarreling among one another about who should say what. The sign for the North Pole got knocked over—three times. And one of the reindeer danced off the stage. Fortunately he was caught by the pianist, which effectively stopped the music and the other cavorting reindeer so they could get themselves reorganized.

Tim loved the performance, but afterward, when we went for refreshments and he saw some of his old classmates from first grade, he suddenly turned shy. The little kids were still in costume and jabbering to one another. Tim stood on my foot.

"Don't you want to go over and say hello?" I asked him.

"No."

"Would you show me who your friends are? Just point to them and tell me their names," I suggested, trying to help him feel as if he still knew these kids.

Tim pointed out one of the reindeer and said his name was Stefan. Stefan's antlered head kept hitting the noses of two bigger kids who were talking to him.

"He looks like a real nice friend."

"Yeah," Tim said. "Can we leave now?"

"Well, first why don't we go tell Stefan he did a great job?"

"He's the one who fell off the stage."

"Oh," I said. "Well, maybe you can call him tomorrow and see how he is."

We left, and Tim didn't say a word on the way home. I wondered if I should try to get him to talk about his feelings. I didn't know much about him or his family history. To me, he seemed like a kid who'd be popular with his classmates, but under the shadow of last year's marriage problems he might have withdrawn. Stefan might have been his only friend, and not much of one at that.

Tim's mood changed for the better once we got inside his house. The home was smaller and cozier than ours, with just a living room, dining room, and kitchen on the first floor. Each room had long, narrow Victorian windows and plain country furnishings, which I liked. Tim took me upstairs, showing me the two bedrooms on the second floor, one with twin beds where he and Ben were sleeping, then led me up a back staircase to a single room on the third floor. It looked as if it was being converted into an office.

"This used to be Ben's room," he said.

I walked over to a set of bookshelves lined with sports trophies. "Are all of these Ben's?"

"Yup. I can read them now," Tim told me proudly, and worked his way down the line. Soccer, basketball, lacrosse, most valuable player, scholar-athlete. Ben had done it all.

I picked up a photograph that showed Ben and another guy grinning at the camera, their arms around each other's shoulders, both of them holding lacrosse sticks.

"That's Lenny," Tim told me. "He was Ben's best friend, but he's in college this year. That book has more pictures," he said, pointing.

I lifted down the scrapbook and paged through, recognizing some of the guys I had seen in the parking lot, especially Twist—he always stood out.

"Why did Ben leave his trophies and pictures here?" I wondered aloud.

Tim shrugged. "He said there isn't enough room in our new house, but there is."

I put down the book and ran my hand over the cool metal of a basketball award. "Well, I guess he's displaying trophies from his new school now."

Tim shook his head. "He doesn't play sports anymore."

"He doesn't?"

"He does homework with me in the afternoon, then, when Mom comes home, goes to work at a store."

What a change from his previous high-school years, I thought.

"He still goes out like he used to," Tim added. "Girls call him all the time."

Just what I wanted to hear. "Well, it's nice that some things don't change. You ready for a game?"

We went down to the living room and played three hands of fish. Then we looked through the Harringtons' library of videos. "Let's watch this one," Tim said. "It's a Christmas movie."

He'd selected *It's a Wonderful Life,* with Jimmy Stewart, which seemed to me a little bleak for a seven-year-old, but Tim thought Clarence the angel was funny. We settled down on an old love seat across from the television.

"I might need some tissues," I said, moving a box to the coffee table in front of us.

"You cry at movies?"

"I do at this one."

"I do whenever I watch *Toy Story*," Tim confessed, then clicked on the video.

Twenty minutes later, after scrunching himself closer and closer to me, he fell sound asleep. He looked younger than seven, his eyelashes curling softly against his cheeks. I lifted my arm and draped it around his shoulders so he'd be more comfortable sleeping against me.

About halfway through the movie I heard a key being inserted in the front door lock. I glanced at my watch, surprised; it was about ten-fifteen, and Sam had said he wouldn't be back till after eleven.

The front door opened, and Ben walked in. He glanced at me and Tim in the living room, then disappeared for a moment, hanging up his jacket. I stopped the video.

"Hope you didn't come back early for me," I called softly to him.

Ben stepped back into my line of vision.

"I told your dad to work as late as he needed to," I continued. "There's plenty of videos to watch. Tim and I are doing fine."

"I can see," he said, coming into the living room.

"So go back to your party," I told him.

He sat down on the other side of the love seat, which made it a tight squeeze with Tim in between. "I guess I'm not in the partying mood." He picked up the cassette case to see what we were

61

watching, then noticed the tissue box. He started to smile. "Do you cry at movies?"

"At this particular movie, yes," I replied, prickling a little.

"But it's got a happy ending," Ben pointed out.

"Sometimes you can cry on the way to a happy ending," I told him.

He looked at me silently for a moment. I remembered what Sandra had said about how by just looking at you, Ben could make you feel as if he were kissing you. I looked away. "I should go."

"Not if you want to see the end of the movie," he said, making himself comfortable, putting one leg up on the coffee table and his arm across the back of the love seat.

"I've seen it several times."

"Me too," he replied, "and I've never cried. But that other one with Stewart, *Mr. Smith Goes to Washington*? My nose turns into a faucet."

I laughed.

"You think that's funny?"

"Yeah, I do," I said.

"Stay, so I can laugh at *you*. Will you?"

I shrugged. "Okay."

He picked up the remote and clicked on the movie. I settled back against the love seat and slid down a little so I could rest my head against the upholstery rather than Ben's arm. Ben glanced sideways at me, smiled, then reached for an old quilt and tossed one end to me so it was spread over the three of us.

I watched the film, wrapped up in a warm and

golden feeling. Tim shifted around between Ben and me, opening his eyes just long enough to look from one to the other, then fell back asleep. Never in my life had I felt so blissfully content. When—without laughing—Ben handed me a tissue and our hands brushed, that content feeling fizzed into an incredible tingling.

Part of me wanted the movie to go on forever, while another part wanted to get the heck out of there before I got truly hooked on a cool guy with a million girlfriends—makeup and big-hair girlfriends who were nothing like me. What had Ben said earlier? *You're a pal.* So what else was new? I'd been a pal to all the guys who fell in love with my sisters.

Of course, the movie did end. Ben hit the rewind button. "I guess I'll have to add tissues to the shopping list," he teased.

"Excuse me? I used two."

He grinned.

"Let's watch another."

We both looked at Tim, surprised. "You're awake?" I asked.

"Come on, buddy," Ben said, "we've got to get you to bed."

"I want to watch another," Tim protested.

"It's too late. Come on, now. Allie will come up with us to tuck you in."

We got Tim upstairs and into his pajamas. He was so tired that he kept walking into things. Ben and I couldn't help laughing. Finally Ben pulled up the covers and tucked them under Tim's chin. Then he leaned down and kissed him gently on the forehead. If the girls at Thornhill High had seen such tenderness, they would've turned to putty.

"Next," Ben said, glancing up at me.

You or him? I was tempted to ask, but I leaned down to Tim, and two little arms wrapped around my neck. "Sleep tight," I whispered.

We headed downstairs without speaking. When we reached the first-floor hall, Ben touched me lightly on the elbow. "Thanks, Allie."

"I wish you'd all stop thanking me. He's a great kid."

Ben leaned against the stair railing. "I'm glad you like him because I think he's got a major crush on you."

"Well, I always wanted a kid brother, you know, somebody to toss a ball to."

"You don't have any brothers at all?"

"Just my two sisters."

"I saw one of them at the party tonight. She—" He hesitated.

"Is nothing like me?"

Ben smiled. "I guess everyone tells you that." He sat down on a step across from the front door, leaving room enough for me, but I remained standing. "I talked to her for a while."

"Which one, Sandra or Julia?"

"The blond one," he replied.

"They're identical twins, remember?"

"Oh, right." He leaned back on his elbows. "I guess that's why it seemed as if she was always around."

I didn't tell him that he might have seen just one who *was* always around.

"It was the sister who came with Mike. You know, Cupcake?"

I grimaced. "You enjoyed that scene, didn't you?"

"It was good for Mike. I like him, but he can get a little cocky around girls."

"Something you would never do," I added.

"I didn't say that." Ben laughed.

"Sandra is the one who's interested in Mike—at least she was as of yesterday. It changes from day to day." I lifted my parka from the hall coatrack. "Julia's seeing someone named Ford."

"If-ever-I-would-leave-you Ford?" he asked.

"Who?"

"He played Lancelot in *Camelot* last year," Ben explained. "When he sang that song, all the girls in the audience fell in love. The thing is, Ford does leave them—flat."

"Well, I'm not too worried. Mike and Ford have met their match. Sandra and Julia know all the games. They always get whatever guy they want."

Ben stood up. "How about you?"

"Me? I play in a different league."

"I should've guessed," he said.

I struggled to get my arms in the holes of my jacket. Ben stood in front of me but didn't try to help. He simply watched me as if he knew he had eyes that could silently hold and kiss a girl. *No big deal,* I thought. *If you don't look at them, they can't kiss you.* But I did look right into those golden browns, and for a moment I stood planted

65

like the hallway coatrack. Then from somewhere deep and scared inside, a voice warned—*Hurt City, Allie. Get out of here!*

"Have to go," I told him quickly, opening the front door.

"Allie—?"

"Hey, here comes your dad." I rushed through the door. "Hi, Sam. All done? I was just leaving. Tim's asleep. Ben got home early," I chattered as I passed him on the walk.

"Ben came home early?" Sam repeated with disbelief. "My Ben? Is he sick?"

I stopped and glanced back at Ben, who was still standing in the lighted doorway, his hands on his hips. "Seems all right to me," I replied. "Maybe he's just tired."

Ben disappeared into the house without a wave.

"Call it a father's intuition," Sam said, "but I think he's caught something. How are you feeling?"

Light-headed, tingly, confused.

"Fine," I replied. "I rarely get sick, and I've had a flu shot."

"That's always a good idea," Sam said.

Yeah, I thought as I hurried to my car. *It's just too bad they can't immunize against hopeless love.*

Seven

THE NEXT MORNING I got up early and trailed my mother around the house, carrying a cup of cocoa and a stepladder, fixing curtain swags and rearranging ornaments at the tops of our three Christmas trees. Aunt Jen called to see if I could meet her at her office in Elmhurst for a run and a quick lunch afterward. At school I ran as part of my training for other sports, but my aunt had done marathons, and I always liked to be challenged by her. I was heading out the back door in my Lycra pants and jacket when Julia came down for brunch.

"How was the party?" I asked, pausing at the kitchen door.

"Great!" Julia replied. "Some college guys came."

"Anybody who was anyone was there," Sandra added, walking in behind her.

"How you'd know who else was there is beyond me," Julia remarked to her twin, "the way you kept orbiting around Ben." She filled a mug with water and put it in the microwave.

"Just for an hour," Sandra replied. "Ben left the party at ten o'clock," she explained to me. "Everyone was wondering why."

Both of them looked at me expectantly.

"Well, why?" I asked.

"I was hoping you'd know," Sandra said.

I lifted my car keys from a hook. "Nope."

She wasn't dragging me into *this* campaign. This time I wasn't helping her out—getting information, carrying messages. If Sandra was in serious pursuit of Ben, the only way I'd survive the holidays was to distance myself from their affair. I started out the back door.

"Did you see that hissy fit Meg threw when Ben left?" Sandra asked, grinning at Julia.

I hesitated. One question, *then* I'd distance myself: "Is Meg the girl with white blond hair?"

Sandra nodded.

"That hissy fit was brought on by you, Sandra," Julia pointed out, "long before Ben left. Meg seemed to think he was her date."

"Well, Ben didn't."

"How was Mike?" I asked, my resolution weakening again. I couldn't help wondering if he'd thrown a macho hissy fit when he saw his "babe" flirting with Ben.

"Funny you should mention him, Al," Sandra replied. "He asked about you." She gave a little shrug. "I told him we didn't think to bring you because you weren't much for partying, and anyway, you were baby-sitting."

"Allie, are you sure you didn't see Ben last night?" Julia pressed.

"I left the Harringtons' house when Sam came home." Technically it was the truth.

Julia removed her cup from the microwave and dunked a tea bag, studying me.

"I'm headed over to Aunt Jen's," I told her and Sandra, then walked out the back door.

As I drove to Elmhurst, I wondered about Sandra's plans. Her show of interest in Ben might have been nothing more than a strategic move in her game with Mike, a ploy to make him jealous. But if the prize really was Ben—and I had the terrible feeling it was—all other interested girls might as well forget it.

When I arrived at Aunt Jen's office, she was dressed in an aqua running suit but still doing business on the phone. She waved at me, and I started pushing back oak chairs, clearing a space in the room. As soon as she finished the call we did warm-up exercises.

"I haven't been running as much as I should," Aunt Jen admitted as we bent our right legs back and stretched. "Men can be such a distraction."

"Tell me about it."

"Oh, really?" Aunt Jen turned her head sharply. "You tell me about it—tell me about him."

"Who?" I said quickly. "There's nobody."

I could tell she didn't believe me, but she let the

subject drop and continued the stretches. "Okay," she said, standing up and patting her jacket. "I've got money for the deli and keys."

"I've got tissue," I told her, rising to my feet.

"Lip gloss." She slipped it in her pocket. "That's it. Let's go."

As was our custom, we didn't talk much the first mile and a half, just cruised along, finding our rhythm. It was forty-something degrees, but the air was still and the sun bright and warm on our backs. By our second mile we were outside the small town, running a hilly road next to golden winter fields.

"Allie, thanks for being such a good sport the other night," Jen said. "I'm sorry our dinner for two turned into a party of five."

"Well, things always get crazy during the holidays," I replied.

"I told Sam he should have time alone with his kids," Aunt Jen continued as we shortened our stride to take a steep hill, "especially when they first arrived, but he decided otherwise. And I didn't want to seem like I wasn't happy to join them." We crested the hill. "Anyway, thanks for making it easier, especially with Tim."

I didn't know what to say. I loved Aunt Jen, but I cared about Tim and Ben too, and I knew this marriage was upsetting them.

"There are a lot of people who don't approve of what Sam and I are doing," my aunt went on. "There are people who make me responsible for his divorce."

"Are you?"

She laughed. "I can always count on you to be straight with me. And to be straight with you," she said, "the love between Sam and his wife died shortly after Tim was born. But they'd decided to continue as partners in raising their children. That arrangement did not become difficult for them until I came into the picture. For that, Sam and I are jointly to blame."

We ran another half mile in silence. "I want to be really happy and positive about your engagement," I said at last.

"But you've already seen the other side of it, the effect on Tim and Ben," she replied.

"Yes."

"Which is the proverbial good news—bad news for me," she added as we reached a flat stretch of country road. "The bad news is your aunt is a villain to your two new friends. The good news is I now have a wonderful link to them, especially to Tim, who has obviously taken to you."

I nodded.

"I asked Tim if he wanted to go ice skating this afternoon and bring along a friend or two," Aunt Jen continued. "I told him we could go to the video arcade or a movie."

"He didn't want to," I guessed.

"Right. The problem is, I need to keep my hand extended to him, but I also have to respect his feelings about me. He has every right not to like me. I'm afraid this is going to be a miserable holiday for him."

"I already told Ben I'd do some things with Tim."

My aunt reached for my hand as we ran and squeezed it hard. "Thank you." She sounded relieved. "I didn't want to impose on you, but I was hoping you would say something like that."

"Love can sure get messy," I said.

"Tell me about it."

I arrived home about two-thirty in the afternoon and found my sisters finishing up batches of homemade cookies. My mother had exchanged her glue gun for an icing brush and was working at the kitchen table.

"Did you see your friend waiting for you on the veranda steps?" she asked. "He wouldn't come in."

"My friend?"

"He's really cute, Allie," Julia said, smiling, "but you'll never be able to wear heels."

"Tim?" I guessed, backtracking to the door. "Tim Harrington?"

"Could be," my mother replied. "He said he's not allowed to tell strangers his name."

"Harrington?" Sandra repeated. "You mean he's Ben's brother?"

I opened the back door and called Tim's name. Sandra immediately got out a plate and started piling cookies onto it.

At my third call Tim came streaking around from the other side of the garage. "Allie Cat! You've got a basketball hoop. Wanna play horse?"

"Okay. But come in for a minute," I told him, "so you can meet my mom and sisters."

He paused just inside the kitchen door, looking shy for about twenty seconds, then said, "I could smell those cookies outside."

"Really?" Sandra replied. "I was just making a batch for you and your brother."

Tim walked over to her and studied the plateful that she was arranging. "We like the chocolate ones best."

Anything that wasn't chocolate was quickly removed and others piled in their place.

"Does your family know where you are?" I asked Tim.

"I told Ben I was out playing."

"Did you tell him where?"

"I didn't know where. Craig, who lives next door, had to show me."

I handed him the phone. "Call home and tell Ben you're here. I'll go get the ball."

When I returned to the kitchen, Tim was up on the stool next to my mother, watching her paint a Christmas-ball cookie into a basketball with a big *T* at the top. Julia was listening to Sandra talk on the phone.

"Oh, it's no problem at all," Sandra said. "I love having Tim here."

I? Was *she* going to shoot baskets with him?

"Tim says he likes chocolate," Sandra went on, "and I could never eat all these cookies on my own."

"Good thing the rest of us are here too," Julia said loudly.

"Look," Tim said, pulling on my sleeve. "Your mom does good art."

My mother glowed, totally charmed.

"Cool," I replied. "Ready, champ?"

"Let me give you our phone number and address," I heard Sandra say as Tim and I headed out the door, "just in case Tim disappears again."

Yup, that's the reason, I thought.

I let Tim start our game to see what kind of shots he could make, if any. Athletic talent must have run in the family, for he had a sweet little layup and was amazingly accurate from about ten feet out.

"Where were you today?" Tim asked as he dribbled around, deciding on his next shot.

"In Elmhurst, visiting my aunt Jen."

He didn't say anything, just got a look of stony concentration on his face, then launched the ball.

"Good one! Go again," I said.

He missed and tossed the ball to me.

"She and I went for a long run together. It was lots of fun," I told him, wanting him to know I liked Jen but being careful not to talk too much about her. "Should we spell *horse* or something longer?" I asked.

"Can we practice layups instead? I need to work on dribbling after I catch the ball."

"Okay."

Tim did layups from both sides, determinedly

working off every kind of pass I threw. After a while we changed places.

"Ready," I called, then sprinted toward the basket. Tim threw the ball too far ahead of me and I had to lunge to get it. I didn't see the tall guy coming hard from my right side—not until after we slammed into each other. But when I realized he was trying to intercept the ball, my game instincts took over. I struggled with him, wrenching it out of his hands.

"Jeez, you fight like a cat!" he exclaimed.

"That's because she's Allie Cat," Tim said, laughing at us.

I glanced up at the dark-haired guy, recognizing him. "Hi, Mike."

"Hello, Allie." He stared at me with those brilliant blue eyes.

I dribbled away from him.

"Do you remember me, Tim?" Mike asked. "I played with your brother last year."

"I remember. You're a forward."

Mike smiled. "Can I play with you guys? Two against me."

"We take it out first," Tim replied quickly.

Mike nodded, then looked at me. "I have one rule."

"Let's hear it," I said.

He touched my hand. "No fingernails. No claws."

Now that annoyed me. I mean, I don't have to resort to such things. Of course, what Mike didn't know is that I always play better when annoyed. And when someone plays me man-to-man and too close, well, as my coach says, "Allie's plugged in." I fake, I run, I rebound like I'm on springs. I was determined to make this guy sweat a lake.

Tim kept up a constant chatter, playing as well as calling our game like a radio announcer. I continually fed Tim the ball, and we were winning by a few points. I thought that Mike's ego might get the better of him and he'd start squelching Tim's two-point tosses to the basket. I even admired Mike for choosing to stick close to me and allowing Tim to succeed.

Which probably shows how naive I am about guys. After all, it was pretty obvious that Mike was playing basketball like a heavy-contact sport, moving with every move of mine, teasing me by dribbling foolishly close. He made a lot of hand fouls that a varsity player wouldn't. But I was so focused on winning, I didn't stop to think about it—not until the game was over and Tim was hopping around victoriously.

"Did you see my last shot, Ben?" he called out.

I turned around to see Ben sitting on the porch with Sandra and Julia, bundled up in their winter jackets and eating cookies. "I saw five of them. They were super," Ben called back. "Hey—coat on, keep your coat on, Tim. You'll catch cold."

"He's strong from the left side, just like you," Mike said to Ben as we walked over to the veranda.

"I know. We've got to work on that right side."

Ben glanced at me and smiled. "You've got to work on the left."

"That's what Coach says."

"Are you coming to the holiday game, Ben?" Mike asked. He stood very close to me. I moved over, but then he moved over.

"I wouldn't miss it."

The two guys started talking about the team's season. My sisters listened with that interested tilted-head look girls get when bored. As Mike talked, *bragged* actually, he draped his arm casually around my shoulders, like we were old sports buddies. I wished I could duck inside and clean up. Julia and Sandra must've known that the guys were coming over, for they had brushed out their hair and applied some eyeliner and mascara. I felt self-conscious next to them. I knew my face got beet red when I played, and I could feel my bangs drying in little salty sticks on my forehead.

"Do you think I can convince Allie to stay in Thornhill?" Mike asked Ben. "We could use her on the team."

"Why not?" Ben said, meeting my eyes, then glancing at my shoulder.

Mike was massaging it now. His hand began to move slowly down my arm. I stood there like a statue, wondering what the heck he was doing. He slipped his fingers between my arm and ribs, still moving his hand downward until it came to rest at my hips. His fingers curled around my waist, pressing against my thin Lycra suit. I saw Sandra watching and suddenly figured things out: He and Sandra were playing a new game, and I was his prop. Well, he really was a cupcake if he thought he could make her jealous of me!

I moved away from him and folded my arms in front of me, rubbing them with my own hands as if I could wipe off Mike.

Ben noticed. "You're going to catch cold," he said, removing his gold jacket.

"No, I'm plenty warm. I wear this suit for sports all winter long."

"But you've got goose bumps," he replied, touching my arm where I'd pushed up one sleeve.

"I don't think so."

He put his team jacket around my shoulders, holding it there for a moment. It was warm, warm from him wearing it. I shivered.

"You don't think so?" He laughed lightly, then turned back to Sandra. "Maybe we should finish the cookies in the kitchen."

"Of course," she said, reaching for his hand to lead him inside.

How could he know—I'd never tell him—that my shivering wasn't due to the weather?

Eight

THE GUYS MADE a big dent in our cookie collection that afternoon. Afterward Sandra headed off with Mike to do some Christmas shopping, and Ben and Tim left to buy a tree. Julia borrowed the Audi so she could meet some friends at the mall up the highway. With my father working in Manhattan that day and my mother keeping a hair appointment, I had the house to myself for a few hours.

I took possibly the longest shower in history, enjoying every minute of it. Then I spread my Christmas gifts out on the floor of my room and began to wrap them. I was fussing with one for my mother, struggling with an overly ambitious bow, when the phone rang. I grabbed the receiver with one hand, the fingers of my other hand having somehow become part of the ribbon I was trying to loop and knot. "Hello?"

There was silence at the other end.

"If this is an obscene call, you're going to have to breathe louder than that," I said.

"Sandra?" a voice asked.

"No."

But before I could identify myself, the guy rushed on. "This is Craig. Craig Smythe. I think you know me, but I'm not sure. I'm in your English class. What am I saying? I mean Spanish. Third row. But I take English right after you do. We pass each other at the door. When I get out of calculus in time, that is. Well, anyway. I've got light hair. Does that help?"

"Help what?" I asked.

"I take pictures for the paper. I took a lot of you in the fall production."

"I think you've got—"

"Which, maybe, you'd like to see sometime," he hurried on. "I mean, I'm sure you already saw the ones printed in the paper. I have a feeling I'm not making too much sense."

You're right about that, I thought.

"Anyway, I was wondering if you'd like to see a movie, maybe after Christmas? Or before? Whenever."

"Listen," I said, "I have to put down the phone for a second. I need to cut the ribbon off this present I'm trying to wrap or else cut off my hand and let it stay as part of the decoration. But don't hang up—I'll be back in a moment."

I laid down the receiver, then extricated my hand from the ribbon and snipped the package free from its tangled-up mess, thinking as I did—*Poor guy, he hasn't got a chance.*

"Hi, I'm back."

"Hi," he said shyly.

"I'm not Julia. I'm her sister Allie."

"Allie? I didn't know Julia had another sister. I'm sorry. You must think I'm crazy."

Yeah—crazy in love. "Not really," I told him, and measured out some new ribbon. "I've answered the phone for my sisters before."

"Maybe I lucked out getting you," he said. "I wasn't making any sense, was I?"

"Well, if I were the president, I wouldn't hire you as my spokesperson." I gathered up loops of the bright red ribbon. "But I have trouble saying things right when something matters a lot to me. Everybody does." I almost had the ribbon under control and was ready to wrap the metal twist around the perfect bow.

"Thanks for saying that," Craig replied. His voice was lower and much mellower now that he was relaxed.

"Well, it's true," I told him. "Darn this ribbon!" I exclaimed as the loops sprang out of my hand. "It looks perfectly tame on its roll, then fights me like a cobra when I try to make a bow."

Craig laughed. It was a warm and friendly laugh. He sounded nice, but I knew he'd have to be cooler—much cooler—for Julia to give him a chance.

"I just buy the ready-mades and stick them on a package," he told me.

"That's because your mother's not Martha Stewart," I replied.

"Your mother's Martha Stewart?"

"No, no, I was just—"

He laughed. "It was a joke. I'm only slow and confused when I try to talk to Julia. I wish I could just e-mail her."

"That doesn't work," I advised him. "Not with Julia, at least. But I'll tell her you called," I added, "and you should call back. She expects guys to do that."

"It took me a month and a half to work up the nerve this time," Craig replied. "Tell her I'll call, oh, sometime around Washington's birthday."

"What if I give you a specific time to call back," I proposed, "and I make sure I answer the phone first. We can talk a little before you talk to her. Will that help?"

I didn't usually volunteer my services, especially since I'd been unwillingly drafted into them so many times at Fields, but he seemed truly sweet, and I could see myself in his shoes. More easily now than I could have last week.

"I'll think about it," he replied. "But thanks. Did you say your name was Allie?"

"Yeah. You better give me your last name again and your phone number."

I scribbled down the information, then clicked off the phone. After tossing aside the uncooperative ribbon, I carried my mother's gift downstairs and searched the Christmas trees till I found a ball that matched. I tied it with a simple bow to my mother's package, snapping off a piece of tree and adding that for the final touch.

When I'd finished all the gifts and placed them under the tree, I returned to my room and slipped out one of my gothic romances from the space between my mattress and headboard. Wrapping a quilt around me, I snuggled into my window seat, enjoying the mystery and the heroine's secret longing for the dark, possibly wicked man she had fallen hopelessly in love with. Except it wasn't hopeless; these stories always ended happily. I needed to be part of a story I knew would end happily.

The afternoon faded around me. I didn't notice that I was reading by purple twilight until a pair of bright headlights swung into the driveway that curved below my window. Sandra was being dropped off. But it was the guy named Twist, not Mike, who was helping to carry her packages.

Not long after, I heard my mother and Julia come in. I stuffed my paperback behind the mattress and joined them down in the kitchen. Both of my sisters were pulling boxes out of shopping bags.

"I was just as glad Mike had to help his father," Sandra was saying to Julia. "Sometimes he acts weird—hi, Al. And I don't need weird when I've got a lot of shopping to do. Twist, at least, is good for laughs."

"As well as a close friend of Ben's," Julia added slyly.

"Oh, that's right," Sandra replied lightly. "I'd forgotten."

"Did you two leave anything for other shoppers?" I asked.

"Tissue paper," Julia said, grinning at me.

My mother came in from the dining room, her hair a new light blond shade, making me think of hay in the manger, which, of course, I didn't say.

"Let's see what you've bought, girls. Oh, my!"

Julia and Sandra pulled out all of their purchases except for what they had gotten for my mother and me. We tried on scarves and bracelets and hair stuff, smelled men's cologne and women's perfume, and handed around CDs. My mother was holding up a pair of glittering panty hose, an arm in each leg, making them dance, and Julia was modeling a red lace bra she'd bought for herself, wearing it over her shirt, when my father came in. He made a hasty retreat to his study.

"You know, Mom," Sandra said, "sometimes I can't imagine how you and Dad ever got together."

My mother smiled. "You girls don't know everything about romance."

"I mean, I can't imagine him asking you for a date," she persisted.

"I asked *him*," Mom replied. "Twice before he asked me back." The three of us contemplated that silently for a moment. *Speaking of impossible matches,* I thought—"Julia, a guy called you this afternoon." I pulled the scrap of paper from my pocket and handed it to her.

"Craig Smythe," she read aloud. "I don't know anybody named Craig Smythe."

"A Craig from your Spanish class?" I prompted. "He sounded really nice."

She shook her head. "What did he want?"

"To see a movie. He sounded really nice," I repeated.

"I know who he is," Sandra told Julia, "and he's nothing to get excited about. You've seen him around—reddish blond hair, medium height, so-so dresser. He's always taking pictures for the paper."

"Maybe I'd better be busy," Julia said.

"Why don't you call him back and find out what movie he wants to see?" I suggested. "What do you have to lose if it's a good movie?"

My mother looked at me with surprise.

"Well, if you think he's so nice, why don't *you* go with him?" Julia asked.

"Really," Sandra remarked, laughing. "This is a hoot coming from a girl who was busy whenever I went out of my way to arrange dates for her."

"I had a full schedule," I defended myself. Besides, I'd gotten tired of being the consolation prize for the guys Sandra turned down. I had begun to suspect that she used me to keep track of them in case she wanted them back.

"Well, if you don't want this guy's number, Allie," Julia said, "I'm throwing it away."

I watched Craig get dropped in with the morning's banana peels. My sisters went back to examining and comparing their purchases. When the phone rang, I was glad for an excuse to leave. I answered it in the hall.

"Julia? Sandra?" the guy asked.

"No," I replied wearily. "Guess again."

"I'm glad I got you," the guy said, his telephone voice soft and deep. "How are you?"

"Fine. Which twin do you want?"

"I want to talk to you."

"I think you're confusing me with my sisters."

"What did you do this afternoon?" he asked.

"Wrapped gifts. Read. If you'll hold on for a minute," I began.

"If *you* will hold on for a minute," he countered.

"Mike?" I asked, suddenly recognizing his voice, though he was making it sound lower than usual, as if he thought it was enticing or something.

"Yes."

"You've got the wrong sister."

"Maybe," he replied, his voice husky. "Maybe."

"Sandra!" I hollered, not bothering to cover the phone. *"San-dra,* pick it up!"

Then I left the receiver lying off the hook and walked away. I had better things to do than be a pawn in their stupid game.

Nine

O N CHRISTMAS EVE, I went for a run by myself, heading away from the last minute
shoppers in town. I could have run for miles on that
crisp, cold day and kept wondering what it would
be like to have Ben beside me. I imagined matching
his long footsteps with mine, striding in perfect
sync, not talking, just being together. And then I
remembered that Sandra was imagining what it
would be like to make out with him.

When I arrived back home, Aunt Jen had come
over and was getting a Christmas tour from my
mother. I could hear them walking from room to
room, Aunt Jen exclaiming over the decorations.
Sandra and Julia were in the downstairs hall, Sandra
standing in front of a mirror, holding her hand up
close to her face, gazing at her image. She smiled at
me in the mirror and wiggled her fingers, making her
left hand sparkle with Aunt Jen's engagement ring.

"Come on, Sandra," Julia said. "You've been wearing it for five minutes."

"Okay," Sandra finally agreed, then slipped off the ring. Julia put it on and held out her hand, watching the diamond catch fire.

"My turn," Mom said as she and Jen joined us.

Aunt Jen glanced at me, but I shook my head. I'd been trying to squelch ridiculous romantic dreams that, since I'd met Ben, were popping up like dandelions. I didn't need to see how an engagement ring looked on my hand.

"Aunt Jen," Julia said, "have you picked your bridesmaids yet?"

"How about Sam's best man?" Sandra asked.

"We're going to think about all that after the holidays," our aunt replied. "Right now we're focusing on my getting to know Sam's family."

My mother admired the flashing diamond on her finger, then handed it back. "Jen has invited us over to the Harringtons' tonight to help trim the tree," she said.

"I don't want to interfere with your plans, girls," Aunt Jen added. "But if you're free, we'd love to have you." She looked at me hopefully, and I nodded.

"Of course we'll come," Sandra said. "What's Christmas Eve without a little kid? And Tim is so cute. I love being around him."

Julia glanced at me and rolled her eyes. I had to laugh.

My mother insisted on bringing food, and Aunt Jen gave up trying to persuade her not to. After Jen left, I was sent to Jim Danner's, an old grocery store on Main Street, to purchase some snacks.

I spent ten minutes circling the crowded lot behind Danner's, then parked the car and walked around to the front entrance. I unzipped my red parka, put a basket over my arm, and started up the first aisle, picking up cheeses, dropping them in.

"Hey, Little Red Riding Hood!"

I turned around. "Hey, Mike."

"Picking up some goodies for Grandma?" he asked. "Mmm."

"Don't get your hopes up, Wolf," I told him. "Both grandmas are dead."

He laughed.

I selected two more cheeses. "What are you up to?" I asked, when he continued to hover about.

"Just picking up some butter." He held it up.

We reached the end of the aisle. "Well, good luck in choosing the fastest cashier line. And have a great holiday if I don't see you."

He took the basket from my hands.

I looked at him funny and took it back. "I have more shopping to do."

He pulled on the basket's handle until I let go, then dropped in his butter. "I figured that. I'm helping you."

"Oh. Well . . . thank you."

Mike laughed. He really was good-looking, his black, wavy hair and dark lashes making his eyes even bluer. He had a movie star face, the kind with very chiseled features—but having nothing particularly interesting about it. He was a good match for Sandra.

"And I'll be seeing you tomorrow," he said as he carried my basket down an aisle of crackers and chips. "Sandra invited me over."

I picked up some multigrains and water crackers, then handed them to him.

"What do you want for Christmas this year?" Mike asked.

"Hiking boots. A sleeping bag. And a pair of good cleats for lacrosse."

He smiled. "No perfume?"

"It makes my eyes water."

"Mine too," he said, "when I get close to a girl." He stood close and looked at my neck, which is long—one of my better features, according to Sandra. I put one hand on it self-consciously, and he laughed.

"You're really kind of shy, aren't you?" he remarked, following me up the next aisle.

"No."

"Well, you're shy around me," he replied with a persuasive smile.

I looked into his eyes. "The word is *uncomfortable.*"

"Why? I don't want you to be." He sounded earnest. "You sure are hard to read, Allie."

"I'm not trying to make it difficult." I put two jars of olives in my basket, lifted it out of his hands, then headed for the deli counter.

"Listen," he said, "I've dated more girls than I can remember the names of."

"That's impressive."

"What I'm saying is, I've had experience. And you're not like the others."

I grimaced. "I think the next sentence is, *I've never felt this way before.*"

He pulled me back by the arm. "No, the next sentence is, I don't usually bother with girls who make it hard to talk to them. I don't have to."

"Unless it serves your own purposes," I replied. "Your strategy is obvious to me." I hurried toward the deli.

"Okay, Allie," Mike said, catching up with me. "Tell me what's so obvious that I'm missing it."

Customers, who were waiting for their numbers to be called, turned around, gazing at us with mild curiosity. I took a ticket and tapped my foot.

Mike faced me, his arms folded in front of him. "Are you going to tell me?"

"I don't like it when people play games with each other. I don't want any part of your and Sandra's game."

"What game is that?" he asked.

"What game?" I repeated, my voice breaking high. I took a breath and lowered it. "You know what I'm talking about. You're not the first guy who's tried it. Though you're probably the first who thought you could make her jealous of *me*."

"Your sister may be playing games," Mike said. "But I'm not."

"Well, you're not exactly acting like a devoted boyfriend."

"What'd she say?" an old man asked.

"He's not exactly acting like a devoted boyfriend," his wife answered loudly.

"I think it's her sister's boyfriend," another customer added.

Oh, man, I thought. *Call number twenty-nine, please.*

"For a good reason—I'm not her boyfriend," Mike insisted.

"Listen," I said, "Sandra's not here, so what's the point? I'm not going to tell her about the way you flirt with me. I'm not going to help you make her jealous."

"What makes you think that's what I'm trying to do?"

I turned away, shaking my head. Mike reached for me, turning me back toward him. "Why are you so sure that's what I want?"

"This is better than the soaps," the old man said.

That did it. My mother was going to have to live without her goose liver pâté. I crumpled up my number and headed to the cashier lines. Then I remembered sodas and made a quick detour, picking up two six-packs.

Mike followed and tried to carry them for me.

"Please, give me a break," I said.

"I've given you several, but you don't seem to catch on."

"I caught on two years ago, when my sisters' boyfriends started hanging around me so they could get information about the twins."

"But I'm not one of your sister's boyfriends," he

argued, "and I think she's made that clear."

"You only have to *want* to be," I said, then got in line.

I guess that point hit home. We stood in line silently through several checkouts that were ahead of us. I started putting my purchases on the belt, and he began to help but didn't meet my eyes.

After I paid for my purchases, Mike caught me by the coat and held on tight while the clerk rang up his. I stood there, unwilling to make another scene. When he let go, I quickly lifted my two bags, which were heavy with jars, bottles, and cheese. He tried several times to get ahold of one.

"This is getting old, Allie," he said as we walked around the building and across the parking lot, still struggling for control, each with a hand on a bag. "Just let me carry one of them. It would make me feel better."

"It makes me feel better to carry them myself," I replied. Then I thought, *Oh, chill out, Allie. He knows you're onto his game now; he's just being polite.*

We relinquished our hold at the same time.

"Oh!"

We quickly grabbed for the bag, knocking our heads together. The slippery plastic slid past our fingers and we tried to catch it again, wedging it between my thigh and his knee. We started laughing, then I lost my grip on the other bag. We both bent at the waist, grasping at the bags, our heads together, laughing uncontrollably. Mike finally grabbed one and straightened up. I got the other and leaned back against a red car—a dusty-looking red car. A Toyota the color of tomato soup.

Then my eyes met Ben's. His friend Twist was standing next to him.

"Need help?" Ben asked.

"No," Mike replied, still laughing. "But thanks. And be careful, you guys. Assisting Allie is a dangerous sport."

"Really," Ben said.

Twist grinned at me. "I'm Twist. Neither of these jerks are going to remember to introduce me."

"Hi. I'm Allie Parker."

He nodded. "I know. You're already famous around these parts."

"Famous for what?"

The three guys laughed.

I looked from one to the other. There I was, standing in a parking lot with three cool guys smiling at me. *If only the girls at Fields could see me now,* I thought. Except that I ruined it by blushing, letting everyone know that I wasn't used to this kind of attention.

The guys talked for a minute more, mostly about basketball and the upcoming holiday game, then Mike helped me carry the packages to my car. As he and I walked across the lot I heard Twist say, "You're right, Ben. It's hard to believe they're sisters."

Ten

"DON'T MAKE ANY sudden stops," Julia told my father.

She, Sandra, and I sat in the back of the sedan, holding our hands up in front of us, trying to dry our nails. And for the second time in four days I was wearing a full face of makeup. Maybe I was morphing. I hoped it wasn't an irreversible process. While we got dressed, I'd wanted more than anything to tell the twins about the events at the store and parking lot. To boast, actually. But I didn't because I thought Sandra's feelings might get hurt. And to be honest, I thought mine might too if my sisters treated it all as no big deal.

It is no big deal, I told myself, *unless you go to an all-girls school.*

"Are the Harringtons on Walnut Street?" my father asked.

"Yes," I replied. "Turn at the next corner."

"Slowly," said my mother. Her nails were dry, but she had been glue gunning on the way out the door, making Tim a wreath with little plastic basketballs. Now she held it carefully in front of her.

We pulled up in front of the tall blue-and-white house and made a parade up the Harringtons' walk, carrying food and decorations. Sam greeted us at the door. "Merry Christmas! Merry Christmas!"

Tim popped out from behind him. "Hey, Allie Cat!" Then he saw the wreath my mother was carrying. "Awesome!" he said.

My mother beamed. "It's for you."

Ben came out from the kitchen area, followed by Aunt Jen and a guy with strawberry blond hair.

"Isn't this cool?" Tim asked, holding up his wreath.

"Very cool," Ben replied. "Hi, Mr. Parker, I'm Ben. This is our neighbor, Craig."

Craig the photographer? The same guy who'd called Julia? I didn't have to wonder for long. He gave me a shy smile but could hardly look at my sister when introduced.

"Craig's parents own the Card & Party Shop on Main Street," Ben told us.

"Which is lucky for us," Sam said. "Every Christmas Eve, while his parents are finishing up at the shop, Craig comes over with everything I've forgotten to buy, like wrapping paper, tape, ribbon, tinsel. . . . It's become a tradition."

I glanced sideways at Julia to see if she recognized Craig as the guy whose number she'd dropped in the trash, but she gave no sign.

"Well, let's take everybody's coats," Sam said.

With the skill of an actress who never misses a blocking tape, Sandra positioned herself perfectly for Ben to help her with her jacket.

I shoved Julia ahead of me so that Craig got a chance to take her jacket. Julia had to help him along, and when he finally saw her in her red silk blouse with a deep V neck, I guess it was too much for him. He took two steps backward into Ben, letting the coat drag on the floor. Then he swooped up the coat, looking distraught, as if he'd been dragging a person. *Poor guy,* I thought once again.

"I'm so glad you're all here," Aunt Jen said as the coats were hung up. "Come into the kitchen. We have cider warming."

We proceeded toward the rear of the house, but Tim held back. "I want to hang this," he said, holding up his wreath.

"Later," his father replied. "Let's get some drinks."

"I want to hang it now."

Ben gave his brother a warning look.

"I'm going to put it on the front door," Tim went on defiantly.

"We already have a wreath there," Sam said with strained patience.

"But I want this one there."

I wondered why he was acting bratty, then Aunt Jen volunteered, "We can put Tim's wreath on the door. It'll look good."

"No," Sam said sternly, turning to Tim. "I like

the one Jen picked out, and it's going to stay right where it is."

My mother looked uncomfortable, as if she'd caused a problem.

"How about your bedroom door, Tim," I suggested, "since it's your own wreath?"

Tim looked at me sulkily. I stared back until he changed his stubborn little expression.

"There's a nail already in the door," Ben said. "I'll get you some string."

A few minutes later Tim and I were hanging up the wreath.

"This looks great," I told him.

"You like her." Tim sounded resigned and unhappy.

"You mean my aunt Jen? Yes. I like her very much," I said, laying my hand on his shoulder.

"Oh," he mumbled.

We'd just turned to go downstairs when the phone rang. The call was immediately picked up by an answering machine in the bedroom. I heard Sam's recorded voice followed by a beep, then a girl's voice: "Hi, Ben, this is me. Come over as soon as you get rid of your guests. Tap on the den window—my parents will be asleep."

"They just keep calling," Tim told me.

Now both of us were resigned and unhappy. We returned downstairs to the living room.

The tree had been put in its stand before we arrived and decorated with strings of big-bulb lights. Jen and Sam were opening up dusty boxes of ornaments, laying them out for us. Tim went over to watch, standing by his father's side, away from Jen. My own father was sitting in the corner, reading the Christmas edition of Sam's paper, and would probably move on to Sam's book collection next. My mother was fussing with the Harringtons' curtains. I wondered if Sam knew what kind of family he was marrying into. Good thing he was a bit eccentric too.

The guys and my sisters were seated on the floor around the hearth, which crackled and snapped with a warm fire. Ben stood up when he saw me. "Can I get you some cider, Allie?"

"Not right now, thanks," I said, joining the group. Ben returned to his seat on the rug next to Sandra, who casually dropped her hand so that it rested lightly on his knee. If I videotaped her, I could have run a sequel to last year's flirting seminar.

"So you and Twist played together even in grade school," Sandra said to Ben. "He's such a nice guy."

"He's a clown." Ben smiled. "We started out in first grade together. Craig too. Craig's family moved next door when he was—how old?" he asked, turning to his neighbor.

"Uh, three."

Ben waited quietly, having provided Craig with an opening into the conversation. "Three," Craig repeated, then fell silent.

"On which side of the road do you live?" I asked Craig.

Before he could get out an answer—and admittedly he was slow in response—Sandra said, "Twist and I went shopping the other day. You ought to see what he bought for you, Ben."

"Some joke," Ben guessed. "He always does."

"I could give you a hint," she said with a teasing look—another video moment.

"You could."

"The west side," Craig finally responded. "I live in the gray house with the rust shutters."

"Do you have a darkroom at home?" I asked.

"Down in the basement," he replied, warming up a little. "I built it myself. I'd be glad to show it to you sometime."

"What's there to see if it's dark?" Sandra asked.

Maybe she was just teasing him, but it shut him down cold. Julia hadn't said a word yet, which was unusual. Maybe she had figured out who he was.

"Okay, everyone," Aunt Jen said. "Time to deck the tree."

"Dig in and throw it on," Sam added.

My mother looked horrified. "Don't you have some kind of decorating plan?"

Sam shook his head. "Just make it stick."

Craig stood up and offered Julia a hand. She looked so graceful rising to her feet that she made Craig look good. His blue eyes shone and caught hers for a moment. I realized then that people can become incredibly attractive when their faces are lit with affection.

"Is it all right if I help myself to some cider?" I asked Sam.

"Sure thing. You're family."

I had headed out to the kitchen when I heard footsteps behind me. "It's okay, I can get it myself," I told Ben.

"You could, but I'm feeling competitive. Is assisting you really a dangerous sport?"

I grimaced, and he laughed. "I've got some questions for you," he said in a low voice, giving me a light push toward the kitchen.

I hoped the questions weren't about his chances with Sandra. At Fields, I had spent a lot of time answering such queries.

As soon as the door swung shut behind us Ben asked, "Is it hopeless with Julia?"

"For you or Craig?"

"Come on, Allie," he said, making a face at me. Then he turned on the stove and began to stir the cider.

"For Craig," I said, "it's going to take a miracle."

Ben glanced over his shoulder. "Do you believe in them?"

"Miracles? At Christmas, I do . . . sometimes."

He turned and smiled. "So do I . . . I think." His dark eyes warmed me like embers. Then he turned back and continued stirring. "I'm not sure whether to encourage Craig. I hate to see him get hurt. You know, he and I didn't really hang out together in high school, but before that I spent a lot of time at his house. He's a nice guy, a guy with a good heart who'd do anything for anybody. That counts for me, much more now than it used to."

Ben stared into the steaming cider as he talked.

101

"Craig is funny and imaginative," he went on. "But he has a hard time being himself until he knows a person, until he trusts a person—especially when he's got a major crush. And does he ever have one!"

I sighed. "I wish I knew how to be his angel and help him along."

"You already have your angel assignment," Ben replied with a smile. "If there's one thing Jen and I can agree on, it's that you're getting Tim through this holiday. Besides, you've helped Craig already." He picked up a cup and ladled in the cider. "He told me he talked on the phone with the nicest girl in the world."

Even though it was Craig's compliment, I loved hearing Ben say it. He handed me the warm glass, and I lowered my head to take a sip.

"Whoa!" His hand caught my chin, lifting it up. "You're going to burn your tongue, Cat."

"Smells good," I told him.

"It's Danner's—you know, the place where you and Mike shopped this afternoon." He looked as if he were going to say something else, then decided against it. "Anyway, as I was saying, you've been helpful enough. Driving up here, I was worried about whether I could still fit in with my old friends. It never occurred to me I'd find a new one. In a way I've found two—you and my old buddy, Craig."

"Good," I said, demonstrating the same large vocabulary as Craig.

"Well, we'd better get back in there and make sure my buddy hasn't tangled himself up in tinsel while watching Julia hang an ornament."

I nodded and followed Ben through the door. Buddy feelings were a long way from the passionate desire I'd been reading about in my paperback romance. I doubted the girl whose den window Ben would be tapping on later was considered a buddy. *Reality check*, I thought. *Just like Craig, you too can get hurt.*

A further reality check came an hour later, when we'd finished hanging the balls. Sandra picked up her earlier conversation with Ben about mutual friends, and Julia joined in. Craig knew who they were talking about but like me was on the outside of that crowd. So we just listened and hung icicles on the tree, one shiny strip at a time. Tim helped us.

"You know it was rude of you," Sandra said to Ben, "to have left Meg at Melanie's party an hour after she brought you."

"She didn't actually bring me," he defended himself. "I drove to her house, and we walked from there."

"But Meg is the one who invited you," Sandra pressed him.

"I would've been asked anyway."

"Oh, really," she teased, "you're awfully sure of yourself. I guess all those stories about you are true."

I looked over my shoulder at them.

"Depends on what stories you mean," he answered. "I've heard a few about you as well."

"You tell one, I'll tell one," she proposed.

He raised an eyebrow. "Ones we've heard about each other?"

"No," she said slowly, thoughtfully, moving closer to him. "Tell me one about yourself that no one else knows." Sandra had the magic of narrowing a room—or an entire gym—to a world holding only her and a guy. She did it with her eyes. I'd seen it all before, but I'd never felt so pushed out. I turned back to my work, just in time to catch Tim climbing the unsteady ladder on the other side of the tree.

"Tim, be careful!" I said.

At that moment he lost his balance and slipped off the ladder, flailing his short arms as he landed and sending two balls flying across the room. A silver one smashed against a table. Tim stared at the broken ball, his face turning pale.

"I didn't mean to. I didn't!" He looked from his father to Jen to his father. "I didn't mean it!"

He seemed panic-stricken. I wondered if the ornament was one of Aunt Jen's.

"It's okay, Tim," she said. "I know it was an accident."

But he still looked upset, as if they wouldn't really believe him.

"Glad you did that, Timmy," Craig said, walking over to him, resting his hand on the ladder. "I've been trying to knock off ornaments all night."

Tim glanced at Craig.

"I've tried three times to crash into the Christmas tree but just keep missing."

The corners of Tim's mouth turned up a little.

"Maybe I'll climb up this ladder and do a one-and-a-half tuck into the tree. Remember how you liked them?"

"Into the pool, not into the tree," Tim said, smiling.

"Just watch me." Craig climbed up several steps, then stood on the edge of one, balancing on his toes so well that I knew he really was a diver.

"No!" Tim said, giggling.

"Didn't you know it's bad luck for the new year if the tree isn't knocked over at least once?"

"No way," Tim told him.

"In fact, my uncle Dave says it's bad luck if you don't throw the tree out the window—from the second story," Craig went on. "You've seen our tree lying out there in the yard, haven't you? That man flattened beneath it is Uncle Dave. Unfortunately he usually goes out with the tree."

Tim laughed and snuck a peek at his father and Jen, who smiled back at him. Then Aunt Jen winked.

Craig climbed down the ladder, not realizing he'd done more than help Tim out of a bad moment. Julia had been watching and laughing quietly and was still smiling now. There is something very appealing about a guy being kind to a child.

An hour later, when my family was leaving, Ben helped me on with my coat. "Maybe there is hope," I whispered to him.

He gazed down at me, his dark eyes glimmering. "For who?"

I pulled my eyes away from his. "You know," I said, and left.

Eleven

CHRISTMAS MORNING I was dragged out of bed by my sisters. We hurried downstairs with as much laughter and excitement as we did when we were little and Barbie dolls were waiting under the tree. My father sat back and watched, looking happy and bewildered: little doll clothes or teenage girl clothes, it was all strange to him. We gave my mother a pile of pretty gifts and my father a stack of books—biographies, history of science, history of anything. I knew he wanted to take his "toys" off to his study and read, but first my mother shepherded us to a church service.

As soon as we arrived home again we were back at our gifts, trying things on, listening to new CDs. I was thumping through the front hall in my heavy-duty hiking boots when the doorbell rang. I opened the door.

"Merry Christmas," Mike said. "I hope all your Christmas wishes came true." His eyes traveled down me, past the hem of my short skirt, down my silver mist stockings to the heavy boots. "I see one has. Nice outfit."

"Thanks. Come on in. *San-dra!*"

"Do you always have to shout?" he asked, but he was laughing. He laid several wrapped boxes down on a table, and I took his coat.

"I think she's upstairs, trying something on."

"Then I'll just go right on up," he said.

"You can try," I replied, hanging his coat on a hook, "if you don't mind my mother lassoing you with a string of Christmas lights, dragging you downstairs, then deciding you look nice next to the hearth—permanently."

He grinned. "This wouldn't be a bad place to live."

"You might not think that when my mother plugs you in."

"Three girls my age," he went on.

"Two. January third I'm out of here."

"That's too bad. Do you have to go back?"

"Sandra!" I called again, but he anticipated it and put his hands over his ears before I opened my mouth. "Faker," I said. "Your fingers were spread out."

He smiled impishly, then took a step closer to me, his eyes an intense blue. He stood close enough to slow dance. "Allie, why do you want to go to a school—"

"Well, here she comes," I said. "I heard her door open."

A moment later Sandra leaned over the second-floor balcony, her golden hair tumbling down. "Be right there!"

Julia came down the steps with her. Both of them wore new skirts and cropped sweater tops. They modeled them for Mike, who turned to me with another of his devilish smiles. "Anytime your mother wants to get out that lasso. . . ."

"I'll let her know," I replied, grinning.

"Lasso?" Julia asked.

"Just a joke," I said.

Sandra frowned a little. "I have your gift under the tree, Mike."

"These are yours," he replied, picking up his wrapped boxes, "one for each of you."

Julia looked at him, surprised. *He's playing games,* I thought. *He's letting Sandra know she's not the only girl in the world.*

"Well, how nice," Sandra remarked without a trace of a smile.

"It is nice," I said, trying to turn the game around, "and clever—scoring brownie points with the rest of us."

Mike blinked.

"Well, let's go open presents," Julia said.

As we walked toward the family room we passed my mother in the living room, fussing with a strand of lights she'd wrapped around a fig tree. Mike glanced sideways at me, and we burst out laughing.

"Same dumb joke," I explained to the others.

Sandra retrieved Mike's gift from under the tree, and Mike had the good sense to sit next to her as she unwrapped the gift from him. Julia and I both waited so Sandra could be the center of attention.

"Oh, Mike, thank you," she said, lifting out a bottle of perfume. "I've been wanting this."

"I know, you wrote down the name for me."

She removed the pretty glass stopper and dabbed her wrists. "Want to smell?" she asked Julia and me, then reached across to us.

"I love it," Julia said, sniffing.

"Mmm," I responded, careful not to breathe in. "It's wonderful."

Mike started to smile, and I bit my tongue so I wouldn't laugh at another private joke. Then he unwrapped his gift, a sports watch, and put it on immediately. Julia and I each opened a pair of earrings. I counted on Sandra to notice that she received something different from our gift, something she'd asked for, so she was special. Julia and I thanked Mike and made a hasty exit, leaving him and Sandra to work things out between them.

"Allie," Julia said to me when we were in the hall, "do you have any idea what Mike's up to?"

"Playing the same games Sandra's playing. Making her jealous, keeping her guessing. Don't you think?"

"Maybe," Julia replied thoughtfully. "There's something else I've been wondering—do you have any idea when a guy finds you attractive?"

"What do you mean?"

"Well, that answers my question," she said.

"What do you mean?" I demanded again. "Julia!"

But she headed upstairs without responding.

*   *   *

110

"Time to strut our stuff," Julia said two hours later.

In years past, when we joined our parents for the holidays, our Christmas celebration was just a dinner for five. But now, living in an area where my father had grown up and my mother attended college, we were going "visiting." After making two brief stops in town, leaving behind my mother's New Year's wreaths and bottles of wine, we drove to a country estate where some banking CEO lived, someone with whom my father's company did business.

The house was a big yellow stucco structure, built in the eighteenth century. Inside, chandeliers hung with greens and long tapered candles doubled their flames against mirrors and paned windows. Men in tuxes played music while others walked around with little silver trays. After my father introduced us to the host and hostess, he and my mother moved on to talk to some business associates. My sisters and I were on our own and stood in a tight circle in the center of a high-ceilinged parlor.

"I don't see anyone we know," Julia said, glancing around.

"Well, it's time we expand our horizons," Sandra replied. "Thornhill is getting a little too small for me. Let's take a tour. There must be some interesting guys here."

The party was spread over the first floor, and we moved from room to room. "Until we've checked out everyone, don't stop, just look," Sandra directed.

"Not even for food?" I asked since we were now in the dining room.

Julia giggled. "This girl stops for chocolate."

She and I let Sandra move on while we snatched up some chocolate creams. When we caught up with Sandra with an extra cream wrapped in a napkin, we made her beg for it.

"Hey, there's Ben and Sam," Julia said, pointing to the doorway across the center hall from us.

Ben was wearing a dark suit and sharp tie. The sophisticated manner in which he nodded and spoke to an older couple made the guys I knew look like Little Leaguers.

"You know the rule," Julia teased, "can't stop till we've checked out all the rooms."

"This girl stops for hot guys," Sandra replied.

Ben and his father didn't notice us staring, but the silver-haired guest did. "Excuse me," he said in a gravelly voice that carried. "I'm sure these pretty girls are waiting for their chance to talk with me."

The man's wife laughed. Ben and Sam turned around, then Sam called us over and introduced us to Mr. and Mrs. Strott. The couple was friendly, asking us how we liked living in Thornhill, what we thought of the shops, the school, et cetera. Despite their interest in us, Sandra kept saying quiet things for Ben's ears only. I did my best to keep up the conversation and cover her rudeness. The result was that I ended up discussing camping areas accessible to senior citizens with a seventy-year-old couple while Sandra led Ben off to the chocolate creams.

Julia and Sam moved on to find Jen and Tim. Mr. Strott and I finished up our comparison of hiking trails, then I wandered on alone. I wanted to find Ben and Sandra, but I was almost afraid to. I didn't want to see them flirting, him becoming another one of her guys, she another one of his girls.

I stopped in a room full of skylights and red poinsettias, a garden room with big windows built onto the back of the house. Except for the flowers and one bench, the room was empty. I could hear the music from across the hall and sat down on the bench to listen. Through the doorway I caught a glimpse of Tim tagging after my mother and waved at him. He changed directions, joining me on the bench.

"What did Santa bring you?" I asked when he sat down.

"I know there isn't a Santa, Allie."

"Me too," I replied, "but he still leaves me stuff."

"I got a cool computer game and a new glove because my hand's getting big. And a boom box. And skates. *She* gave me the skates."

I figured *she* was Aunt Jen. "Sounds like a pretty good haul," I said.

"It's okay." He swung one foot back and forth. "Mommy has other stuff for me in Baltimore."

"Did you call her today?" I asked.

He nodded. "We used to come here with her. I didn't like it because she always made me dance with her."

"She likes to dance?"

"Yeah, and Dad doesn't. He's got a lot of left feet."

"I think two are enough to make it hard," I said. There was a long silence.

"If Mommy was here now, I'd dance with her. I wouldn't whine."

"When you get home, tell her that." Then I had a wild hunch. "Want to dance?"

"Okay."

We rose together. Tim put one hand up between my elbow and shoulder and held the other straight out. "The person with the biggest feet leads," he told me.

"Guess that's me."

Natural athletes move well, even when they're seven. I adjusted my steps to Tim's boy-size ones and danced around the room with him.

"Do you wanna turn?" he asked. "Wanna twirl around?"

"Sure."

We turned in opposite directions, colliding, then pulling apart. Our laughter echoed in the big room.

"Try again," Tim said, "this way." We whirled— once, twice, three times. "Again!" he cried. We spun to the music till I was dizzy.

"Whoa! Stop," I told him.

"Are you going to throw up?" he asked.

"Don't sound so hopeful."

Tim chortled, and a deeper laugh joined his. We turned around to see Ben sitting on the bench. I put a hand out to Tim to steady myself. "How long have you been here?"

"A while." He smiled and stood up.

"So, what do you think—are Tim and I ready for ballroom competition?"

"As soon as you figure out which one is leading," he said.

"The one with the biggest feet," Tim and I responded at the same time.

Ben came over and looked down at our feet. "I win. Can I have this dance?"

I hesitated. "You mean with me?"

"Why would I want to dance with my brother?"

"You have before," Tim said. "You taught me how to do teenage dances."

"Right," Ben replied. "But this is a slow, old song. It's easier to dance to with someone who's almost the same height."

Tim shrugged and went to sit on the bench. Ben slipped his arm around me. I felt his left hand press warm against my back. His right held mine gently, letting my hand rest in his.

"I—I don't really know how to dance this way," I told him.

"It's easy. Just move with me."

Okay, I told myself, *okay. Dance is simply movement and balance.* Only I wished he'd stop looking down at me and start moving.

"Relax, Allie," he said.

Breathe, I reminded myself as we started to dance.

The awkwardness slipped away with the music. We moved all the way around the room, my feet matching his, backward and forward, sideways and around, me always in his arms. I forgot all about being just a buddy, Tim's pal, a funny highway pickup. I wanted to dance close to him. I wanted to be always matching my feet to his, backward, forward—forever in his arms. I wanted to bury my face in the warm place between his neck and shoulder. I heard the slow, romantic music—could hear it inside me.

Then Ben started laughing. "I don't know what song you're dancing to, but the one from the other room stopped," he said.

"Oh. Oh, yeah." I let go and backed away, embarrassed.

He laughed again and pulled me toward him. I resisted, but he held me even tighter. With one hand he gently laid my head on his shoulder. "Come on, Allie Cat," he whispered in my ear. "Hum a song, and we'll dance."

Twelve

WE DANCED UNTIL the music started up again. It was a fast sleigh song and I thought Ben would let go of me, but he held me close and danced even slower than before. I could feel the strength in his arms, the roughness of his jaw and neck against my cheek.

I saw Tim fidgeting, then he rose and left. The realization that I was this close and alone with Ben did strange things to me. My heart started skipping crazily, like the sleigh bell music, but we moved together so slowly now that we'd almost stopped.

"What song are you dancing to?" I asked, trying to laugh, hoping it would cover my trembling.

"The same one you are," he answered, his voice deep, melting me.

He says that to all the girls, I thought. *He knows all the lines, just like my sisters.* And just like their gullible guys, I was close to believing the words were reserved just for me. I pulled back suddenly, afraid of being hurt. "I—I don't think so."

He pulled me to him. "I know so," he replied, his mouth so close to mine, his words felt like kisses. "Close your eyes, Allie."

"Why?"

He laughed quietly. "So you don't go cross-eyed staring at my nose."

I was staring at your mouth, I thought. I glanced past him, struggling to get back to the real world, the world where I belonged. In the room across the hall I saw my parents, Julia, and Aunt Jen looking around as if they were trying to find someone.

"I thought you wanted to be kissed," Ben said.

"Kissed? By you?" If my mouth touched his, I wouldn't be able to hide my intense feelings. My parents and Aunt Jen would see, my sisters would know, and worst of all, Ben would realize I wasn't just another girl to fool around with but a hopeless, head-over-heels case. If my mouth touched his, I might never recover. "No."

Ben gazed down at me, his eyes narrowing.

"My family is looking for me," I told him.

"You know, I thought you were different from other girls," Ben said, keeping me close so that I couldn't avoid his eyes. "But Mike was right—you play as hard to get as your sisters."

I pushed him back, stung by his words. "You think I'm playing hard to get? I think you've got the wrong girl!"

He stared at me, his dark eyes turbulent.

118

"There she is," my mother called. "Hey, Allie, Ben, time to go."

There was nothing he and I could do except act as if we'd been in the middle of a friendly conversation. I heard him take a deep breath and let it out again. We met my family in the center hall.

Sam, Tim, and Sandra stood at the other end of the hall, putting on their coats. "Sandra's coming with us for the rest of our visits," Aunt Jen told me cheerfully. "Why don't you come too, Allie?"

I wondered who had invited Sandra and glanced at Ben.

"Tim would enjoy it," he said stiffly.

"Thanks, but no thanks," I replied. "Tell Tim we can do something tomorrow."

Ben nodded silently and headed down the hall, Aunt Jen following him.

My family and I left soon after. Julia and I rode to the next two destinations in silence, turning on our friendliness at each visit, then sinking back into our own thoughts once we were in the car again. At last we arrived home and wordlessly plodded upstairs to our bedrooms. Then both of us forgot to knock, entering our shared bathroom from opposite doors at the same time.

"I'll use Sandra's," she said.

"No, I will," I offered. "Julia, are you okay? You've been quiet."

"And you haven't?" she countered. She pulled her hair up into a ponytail and began to wash her face. "I guess I've been thinking a lot."

119

"Should you be doing that on Christmas?" I teased.

"Christmas is what has gotten me thinking." She dried her face, then put cream under her eyes and wiped away the mascara. "All the tinsel and stuff. Do you ever feel like you're walking around with a smile plastered on?" She wiped off her lipstick. "Like you're tired of faking it, tired of acting the way everyone expects you to, but you don't know how else to be because you're no longer sure what's real for you?"

"In certain places I feel that way."

"So what do you do?" she asked.

"I leave. I run back to a place where I know who I've always been."

"Fields," she guessed.

"But that's not a good solution," I went on. "I should be able to be anywhere with anyone and be myself." I glanced at my own made-up reflection. "But I'm not. Especially when it counts." She met my eyes in the mirror. "That makes two of us."

About six-thirty that evening Julia put on casual clothes, then drove off to exchange gifts with Ford and meet up with some friends. She asked me to come, but I told her I was tired. Can a person's heart feel tired? Mine did. All the feelings I had developed for Ben that would never come to anything were taking their toll. I was drained.

My father finally got his chance to read, and my mother went up to their bedroom to watch *My Fair*

Lady on TV. I poked through the videos I'd brought from school, trying to find one that would sufficiently distract me from the fact that Sandra had not yet returned. She and Ben must've been having a really good time. I imagined him putting his arms around her, saying, "I thought you wanted to be kissed." She wouldn't get scared the way I had.

I'd just picked out a foreign film from my collection, counting on the fact that reading subtitles would keep my mind off other things, when the phone rang.

"Julia, Sandra, Allie?"

"One of us."

"Allie," he guessed again, "this is Craig."

"Hey, Craig, how was your Christmas?"

"Great!" he said. "I got the Nikon I've been wanting for three years and have been shooting film all day—rolls of aunts and uncles. I can't wait to do some night photography—it's supposed to work well in minimal light conditions."

"I'd like to see your photos," I said. "Especially the ones you took of Julia. Speaking of her—she's not here right now."

"Does she sense I'm going to call and make a quick exit?"

"Just bad timing," I assured him.

"Ben's been giving me a lot of encouragement," Craig said, "and a lot of advice about girls."

"Nothing like getting it from the expert," I remarked, unable to keep the sarcasm out of my voice.

"He's a nice guy, Allie. I know him better than

121

anybody does—know the part of him that kids at school have never seen. You won't find anyone more decent than Ben."

I didn't need to hear this.

"And it has to be tough on him, coming back," Craig added. "He had everything going for him if he'd stayed for his senior year—sports, girls, popularity with teachers. He was the golden guy of Thornhill, you know? His parents knew that and let him choose where to live. But he felt like Tim needed him, so he went to Baltimore."

This talk of Ben and what a great guy he was made me too upset to say anything.

"Are you there, Allie?"

"Yeah," I replied, my voice a little quivery.

"What are you doing tonight?" he asked.

"Watching a German movie with English subtitles about Berlin in the 1930s."

"Alone?"

"How many other people do you think want to see something like that? Sandra's out with Ben," I added.

Then Craig surprised me by asking, "I'd like to see the movie; could I? I won't stay late. I'm helping out at the shop tomorrow morning—it's a big sale day."

I didn't know Craig that well, but what the heck? He seemed like a good guy, and I didn't feel like being alone. "Sure, come on over," I said. "Dress down."

It turned out that we dressed almost identically, in flannel shirts and jeans. I carried a huge platter of chips and dip into the family room while he loaded up the VCR. We kicked off our shoes and sprawled out on the sofa recliners with the chips and remote between us. I felt like I was back at the dorm—stopping the video, munching, talking, starting it again.

I was slipping another video into the machine when I heard the front door open and Sandra's heels clicking across the foyer. "Anybody around?"

"We're watching a movie," I called to her, settling back onto the sofa with Craig. "Second show is ready to begin."

Her footsteps grew muffled by the living-room carpet, then she stood in the doorway. "Oh, hello," she said, seeing Craig. "I didn't expect you to be here."

She sure is good at being rude, I thought.

Then Ben entered the room. My whole body tensed up at the sight of him. He looked just as surprised as Sandra to see the two of us sitting there.

Craig grinned at him. "Hey, Ben! Up for a sci-fi?"

"Whatever you're watching," Ben replied. He wouldn't look at me.

"I don't like sci-fi," Sandra told Ben, as if it were his house and he should do something about it.

"Well, here's what I brought from school," I said, showing them the box, "and here's our home collection."

We ended up watching *Excalibur.* To be more accurate, they ended up watching it; I watched Ben and Sandra. The two of them sat on the love seat. Sandra conveniently leaned back against Ben, turning her

123

head now and then to make private comments, laughing quietly with him. I was about ready to take a sword to her. *Chill out, Allie,* I told myself.

I don't think I was ever so glad to see King Arthur get it through the gut. I stood up at the first movie credit.

"Well, I should be getting home," Craig said, rising with me. "Thanks a lot, Allie. It's been fun."

"Do you need a ride?" Ben asked.

"No thanks. I'm parked on the front street," Craig replied.

I needed some fresh air, so I led him back through the kitchen, picked up my parka, and escorted him outside. We passed Tomato Soup and were striding side by side down the driveway when a car turned in, coming fast.

"Yikes!"

Craig jumped sideways and yanked me out of the way, holding on to me as Julia hit the brakes. She screeched to a halt and quickly lowered her window. "Sorry! Sorry, I didn't expect anyone to be there," she said.

"Don't worry about it," I replied, walking over to her. "We should've been looking where we were going instead of talking away." I had to reach back and grab Craig's jacket to pull him up to the car window. Julia gazed at him with those starry green eyes of hers.

"Hi," he said.

"Hi."

Silence.

"How was your Christmas?" he asked her.

"Okay."

"I hope you got what you wanted and a surprise too. Surprises are important," he rushed on, "because when something good and unexpected happens, it gives you hope."

"Unless it's the wrong kind of surprise," she said.

He looked at me quickly, needing help.

"Craig and I watched one of the weird videos I brought back from school," I said, "and *Excalibur* after that. He was just headed home."

"I thought you were tired, Allie," Julia remarked, sounding a little irritated.

"I was. But when Craig suggested we get together and watch videos, it seemed like a good idea."

"Well, I didn't actually—," Craig began.

I kicked him. "Come on," I said, starting off, "I'm getting cold."

Craig followed me. When we reached his car, I apologized for cutting him off like that. "But I had a reason," I said. "It doesn't hurt for Julia to think you have various girls to call up and hang out with."

"I guess you're right," he replied, "but I've never played those kinds of games."

"Neither have I," I said, "and look where it's gotten me."

"Where?" he asked.

"Nowhere," I told him, and he smiled. "Well, it was fun, Craig. Really. You're a great guy—don't forget that. G'night." He drove away, looking thoughtful.

When I stepped back into the warmth of the kitchen, Sandra and Ben were there, talking to Julia.

"Glad to see you and Craig are hitting it off," Ben remarked to me. "He's a great guy."

"Yup," I said.

Julia looked miffed again, and I was miffed as well. It was bad enough that Ben was getting snared by Sandra; he didn't have to make it worse by pushing me toward his old buddy from next door.

I excused myself and went upstairs. After changing into my nightshirt I turned off my lamp and opened the curtains over the window seat. The electric candle in the window along with the moonlight made me feel a little more peaceful. My gifts were piled onto the window seat, and I looked at each of them again, finally picking up the box from Mike. *Poor Mike,* I thought, opening it, *there's no hope for him till Ben goes home.*

I removed the earrings, then noticed that the tissue had been taped down beneath them in an odd way. With my finger I pulled it loose. Under the tissue lay a chain dangling a small gold heart. A note had been placed beneath that.

"Hope you find this before you throw out the box," I read. "See—I'm not trying to make your sister jealous."

I held up the heart, gazing at it with amazement, letting it sparkle in the candlelight. The hidden gift was very romantic but crazy. I could barely imagine Mike and me as friends, let alone a couple. We both liked sports, but that was it; his idea of a great foreign film was probably one starring Arnold Schwarzenegger.

I slipped the heart and chain back in the box, then heard footsteps and voices on the driveway below my window. I knew it was Ben and Sandra. I didn't want to watch, but I had to.

Ben leaned back against his car, talking with Sandra. She laughed and put her arms around him. There was more laughing, more talking—she was enjoying being in his arms—I knew how that felt. Her hair shone pale gold in the moonlight. I'd never met a guy who could resist her golden hair or laughing green eyes.

And Ben didn't. It was a long kiss—I think. How long's eternity? That's what it seemed like to me.

At last Sandra returned to the house. Ben started to get into his car, then suddenly turned and looked up, gazing right up at my window. Afraid that he might see my face illuminated by the candle, I quickly put my hand over it. Ben stood up straighter. What a stupid thing for me to do! Now he knew for sure that someone had been watching.

I let go and slid down to the floor beneath the window frame, fighting back the tears, losing that battle, feeling like a fool. I guess this was how King Arthur felt, getting it through the gut.

Thirteen

WHEN I AWOKE the next morning, I made a mental list of things to do: Clear things up with Mike, help Julia and Craig, entertain Tim, and—somehow—get over Ben. I had another week left at home. I could moon around and feel sorry for myself or do some things I'd be glad for later.

I called the Harringtons first and was relieved when Sam, not Ben, was the one who answered the phone. He was delighted at my offer to take Tim and a friend ice skating that afternoon. The next item on my list, talking to Mike, wouldn't be quite as easy to handle. Face-to-face was always better, but Sandra was home, so I couldn't invite him over. While my sister was eating breakfast, I snuck into her room, found her red address book (she'd already entered Ben!), and copied down Mike's number and street. Then I pulled on my running togs and headed off, conveniently passing by the Calloways' house on my route.

Actually, I passed it twice while trying to decide what I would say. If his flirtation with me was just a way of getting to Sandra, it was no big deal. Sandra's actions in the last two days had extinguished any concern about hurting her feelings. As for my old rage against guys who might be using me, I was tired of being angry; a guy who'd use me wasn't worth getting all wound up about. But the little gold heart hidden in the box, *that* worried me.

When I'd first met Mike, I readily pegged him as an egotistical jock. Now I wondered if I was guilty of the same thing as some of my sisters' crowd— judging too quickly. Looking back, the scene in the grocery store and the tug-of-war with the bags *had* been pretty funny. I suspected that when Mike's ego didn't get in the way, he was a nice guy.

I had also come to realize that unexpected feelings can spring up between the most unlikely pair—Julia and Craig, for instance. Though last week I would have thought it impossible, what if Mike was actually getting a crush on me? I didn't want the heart of anyone to get as bruised as mine felt right now.

I stood before the Calloways' large green-and-white house for the third time, then sprinted up the driveway and rang the bell. The door opened, and I was confronted with a pretty girl who looked about eleven and had Mike's dark hair and bright blue eyes. The startling thing was there were four younger versions standing behind her. They couldn't stop giggling when they saw me.

"Do you want Mike?" the oldest girl said. Before I could answer, she yelled for him, just like I yell for Sandra.

A minute later Mike came down the steps. "Allie!" he exclaimed. "I didn't know you were coming."

"I guess I should've called first."

"No, I like surprises."

Another chorus of giggles.

"This is Allie Parker," Mike said to the girls.

"I thought her name was Sandra," one of them replied.

"They're sisters," he said shortly. "Don't you all have something to do?"

They gave me mischievous grins and reluctantly headed toward a room in the back of the house, disappearing one by one.

Mike led me into the living room. I'd noticed from the outside that the house had a turret at one corner, and I immediately walked over to the circular area with windows and deep-pillowed benches. Mike smiled. "Girls always like this corner," he said, joining me.

He sat on the floor, then reached up for two pillows, placing one behind his back and one next to him—for me, I figured. But I took a seat on the floor across from him instead. He laughed and scooted over to me. "Lean forward," he said, placing a pillow behind my back. He smiled. "No, you're not shy at all," he teased.

"I'm not," I insisted. "I came over here, didn't I?"

He nodded. "And I'm glad. I get tired of girls playing hard to get."

"Mike, I'm not playing at all."

"Good, then I won't have to," he replied. "Chasing a girl is tough enough without having to wonder whether she wants to be chased."

"I don't want to be chased," I told him.

"It can be fun for a while, as long as it doesn't take too long to get to the kissing." He gazed at me intently.

"I don't think you understand," I said, trying to figure out another way to explain. "I found the chain and heart last night. It's very pretty."

He glanced down at my throat. "How does it look on you?" he asked. "Did you put it on?"

"No."

"Why not?" He sounded hurt.

"Because . . . because I'm not going out with you," I replied.

He laughed and put his arm around my shoulders. "How could you be? I've only known you four days, and for the first three of them I was after your sister."

"Then why did you give it to me?"

"I wanted to. I didn't know there had to be another reason to give a gift."

I was silent for a moment. The idea of giving a gift just because you want to—not because it's expected, and not to get something back—touched me. But still, this gift was a heart. I tried to explain one last time. "Here's the problem. If you've ever fallen for someone—fallen hard—and that person doesn't fall for you, it can really hurt. It can hurt as bad as anything you've ever known."

"I know, Allie," he said, "and I can't promise anything. But I hope you'll take the chance anyway. I don't intend to hurt you."

Hurt *me?* He had it all backward! Or else I did.

"I was wondering," he said, "are you coming to the game tomorrow night? Everybody will be there—we're playing our biggest rival, Elmhurst."

I pulled up both knees and wrapped my arms around them, wrestling with the strange idea that he really could be interested in me.

"Would you come and see me play?" he asked with the earnestness of a little boy. "Allie? It would mean a lot to me."

The things I did that meant a lot to Ben were giving him a hanger to fix his car, taking care of his brother, and helping out his old friend. It was nice to think that simply *being there* for Mike—rather than assisting in some way—really meant something to him.

"Uh . . . sure. Why not? I love basketball."

He grinned. "For once I'll have a girl watching who really knows the game."

I straightened up. He meant it as a compliment, but it always annoys me when guys assume girls know little about sports. "Afterward everyone usually gets together at Bingo's Café," Mike went on. "I'd really like for you to come with me."

I hesitated, then nodded. Why not go where I was wanted?

"It's funny. You can be real quiet," he observed. "You're not big on flattery. But somehow you give me more confidence than other girls do."

"I didn't think you needed any confidence."

"It's a good act, huh?"

"Better than the one I usually put on," I said, smiling. "I guess none of us are sure of ourselves." I stood up. "I better get going."

"I'll see you tomorrow night, then." Mike rose and walked me to the front door. He placed his hands on my shoulders, holding me still, and moved his face toward mine. If I turned away, would he say, "I thought you wanted to be kissed"? I closed my eyes and hoped for the best. *Maybe sparks will fly*, I thought; *maybe the moment Mike's lips touch mine, all my feelings will change.*

He kissed me softly. I stood still as a statue, wondering how the mere brush of Ben's hand could make me tingle all over while Mike's lips did nothing.

Mike smiled. "No, you're not shy," he said for the umpteenth time.

"God, Mike! Just because I don't come on to you doesn't mean I'm shy!"

He laughed, and I hopped down the steps and sprinted off.

I arrived home sweaty and confused. Music came from the living room—ripples of sound that I recognized as piano exercises. I was standing in the hallway, listening, when Sandra hurried down the steps.

"You may want to run a few more miles," she

said, snatching up her coat. "Julia just got started."

"I like hearing her play."

"You always were our best audience, Al." She pulled open the front door. "See you later."

"Sandra!" I called after her. "Wait! I need to ask you something."

She turned back. "Can you make it quick?"

The quicker the better. "Mike, uh, mentioned tomorrow night's game—and Bingo's afterward. He was wondering if, uh, I was going."

"I hope you told him yes," Sandra replied. She didn't bat an eyelash. "I'm sure Julia and Ford can give you a ride to the gym, and Mike will give you one home. I'm going with Ben."

"Oh. Oh, okay." Obviously this new arrangement was just fine with her.

"Well, I'm out of here. I've got to find something incredible to wear for New Year's Eve."

I wondered if she and Ben had already made plans for the big night. I thought about rushing back to Fields and spending New Year's Eve with Miss Henny. But that would be retreating, and I had done enough of that in my life. The best thing I could do was keep myself too busy to think or hurt.

The next item on my list was Craig and Julia. I stuck my head into the living room, and after a moment Julia paused in her playing.

"What's up?"

"Just listening," I said.

"Have a good run?"

"Pretty good," I replied, entering the room. She

135

had music books spread all over the piano. "This looks like major composer stuff. Are you working on something?"

"Schubert."

"Really?" I said. "I thought you were tired of practicing classical works."

"I thought so too. Just like I thought Miss Henny was a teacher too old to know anything. But she was right—talent is not enough. I'm taking lessons again, and in January I'm starting voice as well."

"That's terrific! I can't wait to tell her."

"I'm glad you think it's a good idea," Julia said. "Sandra says I'm crazy, and Ford gets mad because I spend so much time practicing."

"Yeah, well, that's guys for you," I replied. "They expect girls to stand around waiting for them to finish a ball game but get offended when we have our own practice and competitions."

Julia nodded. "Ford doesn't play sports, but he works out in a gym every day. I'm supposed to want to go with him and see how many pounds he can press. But he doesn't want to hear me play, so I don't see why I should watch him push and pull machines."

I sat down on the bench beside her. "I get the feeling Ford's not going to be your one true love."

My sister sighed. "Maybe I want too much."

"What do you want?" I asked.

"Someone I can love and like too, if you know what I mean. I want someone who is really romantic but a real friend as well."

"Maybe you don't want too much—just looking for it in the wrong guys."

"Maybe," Julia replied, her fingers playing silent notes the length of the piano. "So how is it with Craig?" she asked.

"What do you mean?"

"Do you like him?"

"A lot," I said. "He's easy to talk to—"

"When he's with *you*." Realizing she'd cut me off too sharply, she added quickly, "I think it's great he's so comfortable with you. What kinds of things do you talk about?"

"Oh, everything," I said. "He's observant, the kind of person who's very interested in other people. That's probably why he's a good photographer, and it also makes him fun to be around. He knows all kinds of things."

"So, has he asked you out?" she asked.

"You mean on a date? No."

I debated whether to divulge Craig's feelings for her. She must have figured he liked her enough to have called her for a date a few days ago. But she'd chosen to ignore him, and I knew he would seem more interesting if she wasn't so sure where she stood with him now. I decided to give her the all-clear sign from me but not make winning him seem like a sure thing. "Craig and I are friends—buddies," I told her. "You know me; romance isn't really my thing."

"Then why are you reading those paperbacks?"

I stared at her accusingly. "Julia!"

"Well, Allie, you've been hiding stuff in the same place since you were eight years old. Of course, I'm going to look."

"And I trusted you."

"You didn't answer my question. Why are you reading romances if it's not your thing?"

I took a deep breath. "I wish it were my thing, just once." *Like right now,* I thought, *with Ben.* "But all I ever do is make friends with guys or become their consolation prize." I started playing "Chopsticks."

"I've always envied the way you make friends," Julia said. "And I've always admired the way you are with guys—direct. You know how to be yourself, and they really like you for who you are."

I stopped playing. "I've always envied the way you make guys fall hopelessly in love with you. I can't even imagine it."

"Yeah, well, don't bother. Most of the time they're in love with what I add to their image of themselves. They create in their own minds the perfect girl to go with the face, a girl who isn't real—not me. And the terrible thing is, I've let them." We sat side by side, staring down at the keyboard. "I don't know if this is a really depressing conversation or a really hopeful one," I said. "We both want the same thing, so maybe it's not crazy—maybe it's really possible."

"To be ourselves? To have both love and friendship?"

I nodded. "Heart and soul."

"Want to play it?"

We did.

Fourteen

I'D FORGOTTEN ALL about Stefan, the dancing reindeer who fell off the stage, until I took the little boys skating that afternoon. Stefan didn't have much more luck on the ice, and Tim struggled to get used to his new skates. My old, nicked-up blades glided like I'd attached kitchen forks to my feet. We were a dangerous trio. It didn't take long for other skaters at the rink to move out of our way when they saw us coming.

Eventually, despite protests from Tim, I sat down and watched. I knew he needed to have fun with a kid his own age without a "grown-up" between them. Tim and Stefan met two other kids from school, and the four of them became a squadron of planes that didn't always know where they were flying. I let them skate and laugh and shout to the point of exhaustion, then drove the boys home, dropping Stefan off first.

When we arrived at Tim's house, he told me,

"You've got to come in. I have a present for you."

"I would even without a present."

"You'll like it," he said as I trailed him up the walk. Tim pushed open the front door and dropped his skates with a clatter. "I'm home!"

"No kidding," Ben called from upstairs.

"Did you bring back both legs?" I recognized the voice as Craig's.

"Yeah, and Allie too."

I hung my coat over the banister and followed Tim into the living room. "Let's look at my gifts first," he said, then showed them to me one by one, explaining how to use them. I kept missing the details, distracted by the presence of Ben in the house. When Tim tried to explain some mixed-up rules for a board game, I had to focus as hard as I did in math class.

"Get it?" Tim asked me. "Get it?"

I stared down at the colored squares, listening to footsteps on the stairs. "Sort of."

"Hey, Allie," Craig greeted me, coming into the living room. "Hi, Tim. Hi, Ben."

I wasn't sure what I'd see in Ben's eyes. The turbulent, angry look they held after we had danced on Christmas? Or laughter because he'd caught me spying when he kissed my sister? "Did you give Allie her present yet?" Ben asked.

Nothing. There was nothing in his eyes, which was worse than what I'd imagined. I was just a person visiting his little brother.

Tim crawled under the tree, then squirmed out again and handed me a box.

"Wow! Did you wrap this yourself?" I asked.

He nodded. The paper, which had footballs and cartoon characters all over it, didn't quite make it around one end of the box. A stick-on bow had been placed in the bare spot and another one on top.

"I taught him all my wrapping tricks," Craig said, grinning. He and Tim stood next to me as I tore the paper. Ben kept his distance.

I lifted the lid and pulled back pieces of tissue. A furry leopard head emerged—two of them—slippers in spotted fake fur with big leopard heads on the toes.

"Wow!" I said, pulling them out. "These are . . . incredible."

"You like 'em?"

"Of course!"

"Leopards are cats too, Allie Cat," Tim told me. "That's what Jen said. They ran out of Garfield."

"Leopards are much cooler," I said, removing my shoes and pulling on the slippers.

"Jen said you have the same size feet as her."

"I do. These are perfect." I got up to model them for him, doing some fancy turns, then wriggling my toes. "They feel real comfy," I told him, sitting down again to take them off. "Thanks, pal." I held out my arms and gave him a big hug. He squeezed me tight. Over Tim's shoulder I saw Ben watching, his face expressionless.

The phone rang, and Ben turned away to answer it. A moment later he said, "It's for you, Tim. Who's J. R.?"

"A kid from my class last year. He was at the skating

141

rink. I'll take it upstairs," he added, in what I thought was Tim's imitation of Ben wanting his privacy.

When Tim had disappeared, Ben said, "He saw some kids he knew at the rink?"

"Yes, J.R. and his friend Kevin."

Ben sat down across from me and stretched his long legs out in front of him. "I was hoping something like that would happen. I appreciate you taking him, Allie."

"It was fun," I told him. "Tim mentioned Jen twice. Is that going better?"

"I think so. When he decided to get you a gift this morning, he let her drive him to the mall."

"Great!" At least I could still talk to Ben about Tim. Nothing would change that.

Craig sprawled comfortably on the rug between Ben and me, leaning back, propping himself up on his elbows.

"Craig just showed me some pictures of Julia—photos he'd taken at the fall production," Ben said.

Craig and Julia, another "project" we shared. "Yeah?"

"They're terrific," he added, then glanced at Craig, who looked as if he were going to deny it. "Don't argue," Ben told him. "They are some of the best I've ever seen. They have—I'm not sure how to put it—a sense of a real person behind the face."

"A person with heart and soul?" I suggested.

He nodded.

"I could give them to you, Allie, to give to Julia," Craig offered.

"Not yet," I told him. "And you should be the one to give them to her. Just not yet."

I saw Ben tilt his head, one side of his mouth curling a little. Had I said something funny?

"The thing is, I don't know what to do next," Craig said. "I don't have a good excuse to see her. We can't decorate the tree again."

"We can take down the tree," I replied. "Or you can come over for another of my strange videos from school. You can show me how to shoot good pictures—I'll make Julia model. We can, I don't know, there must be a million ways to get you two together. I just have to figure out which is best and in what order."

I heard Ben laugh.

"Julia is getting back into classical music again," I went on, "and taking it seriously. She's practicing piano and is starting voice lessons in January. File that away for future reference."

The sardonic smile on Ben's face was getting to me. "What?" I asked him, prickling. "What's the problem?"

"The Parker sisters should open a dating consulting firm," he replied. "You and your sisters know all the maneuvers. You can coach the rest of us."

"The practices would be fun," Craig noted cheerfully.

"I don't know if guys would have the endurance it takes," I commented.

"Oh, I think we would," Ben answered smoothly. "At the end you could test us at rest stops on the Jersey Turnpike."

That stung.

143

"You know what, Ben? You know what would do you a lot of good?" I said. "To fall head over heels with a girl you can't have."

The smile on his face disappeared.

"To fall in love—I mean really, incredibly in love—with someone who isn't interested in you, and see how that feels." I forced myself to meet his eyes steadily, making him look away first.

"Well." After a moment Ben stood up. "Can I get anybody a soda?"

"Uh . . . I'll take one," Craig said when I didn't reply.

Ben went out to the kitchen. I rubbed my head, then felt Craig patting my foot.

"Got a little intense, didn't I," I murmured.

"A little," Craig said gently.

We sat quietly, which was something I could feel comfortable doing with Craig. If Julia and he ever got together, she'd find out how nice that was.

"Craig," I said after a few minutes, "will you be photographing tomorrow night's basketball game?"

"I cover all of them."

"Julia will be there. Afterward everyone's going to Bingo's. Julia's going with Ford, but don't let that bother you. He's sinking fast."

"Bingo's is where the team hangs out," Craig said.

"Right. I'll be there with Mike."

"You're going with Mike?" he repeated, clearly surprised.

Ben had just come back into the room. "Yeah, well, it's a long story," I muttered.

Ben set down three sodas. "I brought an extra

in case you wanted one," he told me.

"Thanks. Can I take it with me?" I asked, rising. "I really have to get going."

"Sure."

"Anyway, you should come, Craig," I told him as I walked to the hall to get my coat. The guys followed me, Ben carrying my soda. "A lot of kids will be there, and I'll hardly know anyone."

"Allie," Craig said, "Bingo's is where the team and their friends hang out."

"Yeah, so?"

"I'm not part of that crowd."

"Like I am?" I laughed. "I've never been part of a cool crowd in my life."

"You are now," Ben interjected, handing me the soda can. "The captain of the basketball team has made you part."

He sounded angry, as if I'd been given a free pass to a social scene where he didn't think I belonged.

"Mike invited me to join them for one night," I said. "And I agreed. Lucky *him!*"

I opened the front door, strode down the walk to my car, and drove off with my head held high.

Oh, I was cool, I was a girl who knew what she was about and where she was going. . . . I just didn't happen to notice right then that it was snowing like crazy. A blizzard was blowing, and I didn't even turn on the windshield wipers, not until I pulled into our driveway and realized I couldn't see three feet past the hood of my car. I flopped against the steering wheel, my heart aching, wishing like anything it was January third.

Fifteen

HIGH WINDS AND snow made it impossible for anyone to go out Saturday night. As the snow fell, Julia shifted from piano exercises and Schubert to love songs—long, sad love songs that made me crazy. Then Sunday morning Sandra put me in an even better mood by modeling outfits she might wear New Year's Eve. Sometime the previous evening, while I was finishing my paperback romance, Sandra had called Ben and asked him to go with her to Twist's big year-end party. He, of course, said yes.

By noontime Sunday the storm had tapered to flurries. I spent the afternoon clearing the walk and driveway and would have happily shoveled all the roads in town as an excuse to be away from the house. But the basketball game was that night, and I eventually had to come inside to take a shower.

At dinner my mother passed around overcooked chicken and said how delighted she was that I was going to the game with my sisters. Then I informed her I would be meeting Mike and Sandra was going with Ben. She looked confused.

"That's a terrible arrangement," she said. "When the holidays are over, you'll all end up miles away from each other."

"It's safer that way," my father remarked.

"I already have Ben's e-mail address," Sandra told everyone. "And I can stay with Allie on weekends."

I choked on my chicken, then gulped down some water. "You can stay with Miss Henny."

She smiled at me. "You don't really mean that."

"I do mean it. My room's small, and I've got my own life at school now."

"How fortunate for you," Sandra said coolly, "that I didn't try to keep you out of my life at my school. You sure managed to land yourself in the middle of things."

"I didn't try to."

She gave a little shrug. "Well, in the end you did me a big favor, getting me off the hook with Mike. Not that I ever really encouraged him," she fudged, "but I hate to disappoint guys who want to date me."

"One of the tragedies of your young life," I muttered under my breath.

"Funny how things turn out for the best," Sandra said. "All's forgiven, Al." She breezed upstairs to make herself more beautiful, if that were possible.

"You don't look too happy for someone who's just been forgiven," my father observed.

I glanced up from my plate, blinking away my

miserable mental image: Ben and me in Fields's waiting parlor, making small talk, while Sandra finished dressing. Out of the corner of my eye I saw Julia shake her head at Dad. The subject was dropped.

Ford picked up Julia and me at seven o'clock. I hadn't gotten a good look at him my first day home, but I could see now that with his blond hair, gray eyes, and high cheekbones, he was a guy with a future in soaps.

When we arrived at the school gym, a mob had already gathered for the traditional holiday game. In small towns like Thornhill, not just students but adults and little kids show up to cheer on their team. People had brought homemade signs. Foil streamers and pom-poms in Thornhill's gold and Elmhurst's scarlet floated, shook, and shimmered. Music blared. The game hadn't begun, but the place was already rocking.

Both teams were warming up. As the three of us made our way along the sidelines, looking for an empty space in the stands, Caroline, the twins' friend, caught me by the arm.

Her red hair looked like a lion's mane tonight. A big *T* stretched over the chest of her cheerleader sweater and narrowed down to her waist, where a short gold skirt with blue pleats flared over full hips. "Hey, girl," she greeted me.

"Hey, Caroline! You look terrific."

"Thanks. You know we'll do our best, Allie, to cheer him on."

"Him?"

"Everyone," she called to the other girls on the squad, "this is Allie. Allie Parker." They gathered around.

"Julia and Sandra's sister," I explained.

"Oh, really?" a dark-haired cheerleader replied. "I didn't realize that."

"We wrote a new cheer for Mike," another girl told me.

"Well, that's nice," I said. It wasn't until I walked away that it sank in: I was not being introduced as the twins' sister but as Mike's date.

Julia and Ford had gone ahead and claimed part of a bench in the stands. I climbed up after them.

"They got a great turnout," I said.

"Everyone in this town shows up for sports," Ford remarked. "It's the one thing they can all understand."

I glanced around the gym. "There's Craig," I said, standing up and waving to him, but he was busy taking pictures. Tim, who was sitting with his father and Aunt Jen, saw me and waved back from the next set of stands. Before he could squirm his way over to us, his father collared him.

As people squeezed into the packed gym it was becoming more and more difficult to hold on to seats for Sandra and Ben.

"Isn't your sister ever on time?" Ford complained.

The teams lined up to be introduced. The announcer called the names of the visiting team first and for each team the bench players before the starting lineup. When everyone on the home team but Mike had run out to the center and high-fived his mates, the announcer finally called out, "Starting at forward, Thornhill's team captain, senior, number ten, Mike Callowaaaay!" The gym erupted.

It was weird, totally weird, feeling the bleachers vibrate, having hundreds of fans cheering around me, drums beating, girls waving their pom-poms for the guy who would be driving *me* home tonight. I felt as if I'd taken over some other girl's body.

We stood for "The Star-Spangled Banner," facing toward the flag that hung at the far end of the gym. Julia elbowed me as the anthem started. "Mike's looking for you."

Mike and I turned and saw each other at the same time. He continued to gaze up at me, and I flicked my head in the direction of the flag, signaling to him that he was supposed to be looking that way. He just smiled.

Then Ford twisted around next to Julia, searching the rows behind us. "Why does that photographer keep looking up here?" he asked.

"Do you mean Craig?" I replied, glancing sideways at Julia.

She shrugged.

The anthem ended, and the starting players took their positions. Caroline and her squad raised their pom-poms. *Jump ball, jump ball, hey hey hey!*

I knew most of the cheers and was in the mood for hollering. A few minutes later Janice, the striking, dark-haired girl from the drama club, scrambled up beside the three of us. "What a mouth you have!" she said to me. "We could use her in the spring production, Julia."

It was a good game, the score seesawing back and forth. Mike played well—not exciting basketball but very solid. Twist turned and faked and spun with the ball, demonstrating where he got his nickname. I was really enjoying myself, and only Ford seemed annoyed by my cheering, which had become contagious.

Then the ref made a bad call, a real stinker against our team.

"Go see an O.D.!" I called out.

"An O.D.?" Janice asked.

"An eye doctor—in Latin, I think."

"Go see an O.D.! Go see an O.D.!" the chant went up from our section.

Janice and I were swinging our hips, leading the crowd, when all of a sudden Ben came up beside me. Sandra was on the other side of him.

"Having a good time?" he asked me.

"Oh, yes!"

"You'll go deaf," Sandra warned Ben. "Allie cheered for me the year I went out for JV basketball."

"I wasn't cheering for you, Sandra, I was yelling directions."

Ben laughed.

"We were afraid you wouldn't find us," Julia called over the roar of the crowd. "When did you get here?"

"The national anthem," Sandra replied.

"That's how we found you," Ben added. "I saw Mike and Craig turned this way and turned with them, thinking Old Glory was hanging up here."

We got back into watching the game, and I continued to cheer. I had to if I wanted to stay sane. Each bump of Ben's arm sent sparks through me, and being squeezed together there on the bench, we bumped a lot. Sandra wanted the seat on the end so she could run up and down the bleachers, saying hello to friends. Every time she left, my heart started thumping the way it had when I realized Ben and I were dancing alone. Somehow the eight hundred other people in the gym didn't seem to matter.

"Calm down, Allie," I mumbled to myself.

"Did you say something?" Ben asked.

"No. No."

"Yes, you did," Janice whispered to me from the other side.

"I just don't get it," Ford said. "What is it that makes girls so crazy about jocks?" He was watching the girls two rows in front of us checking out the players. "We make heroes out of a group of guys who bounce a ball and throw it through a hoop. I mean, look at our school photographer." He pointed to Craig. "You'd think he was covering the NBA play-offs."

Craig had been snapping pictures energetically during the first two quarters, getting down on his stomach, up on a stepladder, oblivious to everyone and everything but what he was shooting.

"That's how a photographer works," Julia said. "He takes lots of pictures to get one or two perfect shots."

"Craig covered us in the fall production that way," Janice reminded Ford, "and got some great photos."

"And covered the kids in the town's Halloween parade that way," Ben added, "and the shop owners at Christmas. It's not only jocks Craig pays attention to—he finds anyone an interesting subject, except maybe himself."

"Which is why I find *him* interesting," I said.

Having finished the sales pitch, Ben and I glanced at Julia, then at each other. He smiled a little. We were still connected by our hopes for her and Craig. But I let the momentary connection go too long; Ben must have seen something else in my eyes, for as he looked at me his eyes changed. The gaze, the warmth that made them like embers, was suddenly there again.

Then the halftime horn blew and we both looked away.

I guess everybody in high school dreams of making an entrance with either the school hero or hottest girl around. After the game I achieved that dream at Bingo's Café, and frankly, it's not all it's cracked up to be.

Maybe the self-esteem stuff Fields's teachers have been pounding in our heads has given me a false sense of my own importance, but it really annoyed me to be viewed as nothing but "Mike's new girl." Why wasn't he "Allie's new guy"? Of course, his crowd knew him, not me, but what bothered me was that no one there wanted to know me. Everything I was asked that night related to Mike:

What did he give me for Christmas; what did I think of the game he'd just played; what were his and my plans for the rest of the vacation?

Bored, I picked up my soda and french fries, hoping to have a real conversation with Craig. Ben had convinced his old friend to come, but he was sitting at a booth on the edge of the in-crowd gathering, talking to people who weren't part of the group. I started in his direction, then Mike caught me by the arm.

"Allie," he said, "are you going with me to Twist's New Year's Eve party?"

I gazed down at him with surprise. Maybe this was dream number two of high school, being asked on the big date by the school hero in front of others. But I felt trapped. Ben, who was sitting at the next table with his arm draped around Sandra, was watching and listening for my answer—a lot of people were. Why would Mike risk rejection in front of them? Unless, of course, he was sure I would say yes.

And the truth was I wouldn't embarrass any guy by turning him down in front of his friends, especially on his big night. "Sure," I said.

Mike took my soda and fries from me and pulled me down into the seat next to him. Ford sat across from us. "I've hardly had a chance to talk to you since the game," Mike said.

"That's okay," I replied. "You're the star tonight and have lots of friends to see."

He put his arm around me. "You're a sweet girl."

I grimaced, and he laughed. "Okay," he said, "pretend you're not."

"I don't have to pretend."

"Did you ask Allie about Tuesday night?" Julia asked, coming over to our table. She sat down next to Ford. "I couldn't remember if you had something to do, Allie."

It was an old warning system devised by my sisters and me, a way of giving the other person advance notice in case she wanted to wiggle out of an invitation. Usually, however, *I* wasn't the one who needed time to think up an excuse.

"Julia and I are going up to Windhaven for the Boat Light Parade," Ford told us. "It starts at six o'clock. Afterward we can walk through Windhaven Park. My parents have a cabin there, and we can hang out. They won't be around, of course."

"Sounds cool," said Mike. "We're free Tuesday night."

"How do you know I am?" I asked.

Mike laughed. "Because I haven't asked you to do anything else yet."

"That only means *you're* free."

He looked confused for a moment, then grinned. "You're right. You're not sweet."

"So are you coming, Allie?" Ford asked.

I thought for a moment or two, longer than I needed. "Okay."

Ford glanced over at Sandra and Ben. "You guys are welcome too," he said.

"No thanks, we already have plans," Ben replied, which made me feel both relieved and miserable.

For the next hour I tried to keep my focus on

Mike. After all, he was the one who wanted me around. As he drove me home from the café we talked a little, then lapsed into silence. I figured that the hard-played game was catching up with him.

"You look tired, Mike," I told him when we pulled into the driveway. "I can walk myself to the door. Don't get out in the cold."

He unbuckled his seat belt. "Stay here where it's warm," he said, and put his arms around me. He pulled me close to him, turning my face toward his.

His eyes were an incredible blue, his mouth as sensuous as a guy's in a cologne ad. He sure would have looked good hanging in a gym locker at Fields. *Maybe this time,* I thought. *Maybe this time I'll feel something.*

We kissed. A short kiss, then a longer kiss, then one that felt as long and wet as the Mississippi. I waited for fireworks. I would have settled for a glowing cinder. Nothing.

Right when I was about to pull away, the two of us were frozen like two deer in the headlights of a car.

Mike drew away, laughing as the headlights were quickly extinguished. "Guess we've been caught," he remarked.

"Yeah," I said, laughing with him. "Well, good night."

I kept a smile on my face all the way to the back door. The headlights that had illuminated us belonged to Ben's car, and if I didn't keep laughing, I'd cry.

Sixteen

MONDAY MORNING WAS one of those blue sky, white snow days, when the sun is brilliant and the snow dazzling and you can hardly wait to get outside. Tim called, asking if I wanted to go sledding. An hour later I found him waiting on his front steps, holding the ropes of an old runner sled and a snow tube. "I know the best hill. It's a long walk, but we can make it."

We walked three blocks to the end of Walnut Avenue. I dragged the sleds while Tim ran ahead and slid on every gleaming patch of sidewalk ice he could find. The street ended in a field of snow that was about eight inches deep, a gradual uphill climb stubbled with high grass. Tim pointed me in the right direction and told me to go first. "Ben always goes first so I can walk in his footsteps."

"There are some footprints over there." I pointed.

"Those are Ben's from yesterday, when he

mashed down the snow to make a good run for my sled. But he went the long way."

At the end of the field we walked through a stand of windblown pine, then looked down over a long sweep of hill. "Perfect!" I said. "It's absolutely perfect!"

"Do you want the runner sled or the tube?" Tim asked, dancing around.

"How about if we switch back and forth?"

He plopped down in the tube. I gave him a push and listened to him screech and holler all the way down. When he stood up and signaled that he was clear of the path, I set the runner sled in the track. I felt like a little kid again, getting a running start, flying down the hill on my belly, the wind and snow in my face.

"Your eyes are really shiny," Tim told me six or seven runs later. "And there are snowflakes in your hair."

"Then we look alike," I said, pulling my ski hat down over my ears and pulling down his too.

We rode the runner sled together several times, sitting toboggan style, racing each other up the hill after every run, panting and slipping and throwing snow. On one of those trips uphill the snow tube zipped past us.

"It's Ben!" Tim exclaimed happily.

My heart quickened. When the tube reached the bottom of the run, Ben turned to wave at us. Tim sidled close to me, forming a snowball in his hand.

"Don't let him up the hill," he whispered.

"Right," I said, and scooped up some snow.

"Make as many as you can. We'll need extra power."

I packed three more snowballs. "You give the signal, sir," I told him.

We watched Ben making his way up the hill toward us. He must have known what was coming, but he pretended not to.

"Ready," Tim said. "Aim." He lifted his arm. "Fire!"

We pelted Ben with snowballs and snow blobs, hastily making more as he dropped the snow tube and armed himself. He was a good shot, and Tim and I had to duck and skip despite the advantage of being uphill.

"Fire! Fire!" Tim kept shouting.

When Ben was about fifteen feet away, he got me with a snowball hard on the arm.

"Yow!"

"Don't give up," Tim cried.

"I have not yet begun to fight!" I exclaimed, quoting somebody or other.

Ben laughed and leaned over to scoop up more snow. I reared back and threw. Bull's-eye! It wasn't really what I was aiming for, but I got him—right on the butt.

Ben straightened up slowly.

"Oops," I said with a smile.

Tim laughed hysterically.

Ben just looked at me, then started to walk slowly toward me, not saying a word, shaping a huge snowball in his hand.

"I think it may be time to retreat, sir," I said to Tim.

"Retreat!" Tim shouted.

We scrambled up the hill, tripping in the heavy snow, trying to pull the sled with us. I felt my feet go out from under me. Ben had ahold of my ankles.

"Help, Tim!"

Tim ran over and tried to pull me uphill by the arms. I went down on my stomach in a mound of snow.

Ben flipped me over on my back—a little too gently for a guy bent on revenge—and began dragging me down the hill. I held on to Tim and dragged him. He laughed all the way.

At the bottom of the hill Ben dropped my ankles and stood over Tim and me. "Now try to get up," he said.

"Conference, Tim." I squirmed around on my back so I could whisper to him. "We'll have to fake him out," I said, cupping my hands over my mouth. "Pretend to go for Ben's ankle, and when he starts to react, jump up. Then I'll get his other ankle."

"Then we'll smother him with snow."

"Right."

Tim executed the plan perfectly, snatching at Ben's ankle, then springing to his feet. I gripped the other ankle, hanging on like a mad dog, and pulled. Ben went down on his rump. Snow flew. We were like three people splashing in a pool, making waves, with fountains of snow shimmering down on us.

I laughed till my sides ached and lay back in the

snow exhausted, still laughing. The brilliant sunlight seemed as if it were dancing in my eyes. I listened to Ben's deeper laugh and Tim's bright giggles till the three of us finally quieted down. Staring up at the high blue sky, I was content to the tips of my toes.

A minute or two later Ben stood up and pulled Tim and me up with him. "You're nothing but trouble," he said, "both of you."

"There wasn't any trouble till you came," I replied.

We climbed the hill, retrieving our sleds on the way.

When we arrived at the top, Tim wanted to ride double decker on Ben's back. I gave them a push-off, then took the snow tube down by myself. We made the same run several times, and I experimented with shifting my weight to make the tube spin. When Tim saw me whirling around, he wanted to try it.

Ben and I launched him, then Ben held the runner sled in position. "Do you want to go by yourself or with me?" he asked.

I hesitated, then told myself not to make a big deal out of nothing. All he'd asked was if I wanted to share the sled. "I'll go with you."

"Double decker?"

I nodded.

He lay down on the sled, and I lay down on top of him.

"You're going to have to hold on tight, Allie," he said. "The upper deck always gets the bumps and turns worse. Can you loop your feet around mine?"

My legs were shorter, so I hooked them just above his ankles. I was glad that there was enough fiber fill between us to keep him from feeling my beating heart.

"You're not afraid to hold on to me, are you?" he asked. "If you are, I'm going to lose you halfway down the hill."

I pulled myself forward two inches, rewound my feet, dug my fingers into his shoulders and jammed my chin down on his neck. "How's that?"

"Better," he said, laughing. "Just keep your mouth closed when we start. I don't want to get bitten."

He pushed off with his strong arms.

"How can I keep my mouth closed when— whoa—*ooo*—*oah!*"

We went flying down the hill—I think he was steering crazily on purpose—swerving left and right, hitting a big bump.

"Ow!" I screamed in his ear but hung on tight.

We swerved past Tim, who was pulling his tube up the hill, and shot over an icy patch.

"Cripe!" I exclaimed.

"Hang on!"

We swerved again and at the bottom of the hill whipped around in a hockey stop that threw us sideways off the sled. Ben tumbled after me, rolling on top of me. For a moment neither of us spoke.

"Are you okay?" he asked.

Having Ben on top of me, gazing down at me with his face six inches from mine, had a devastating effect on my memory of English. He slipped one arm under my back and a hand under my head, pillowing it in the snow. I had lost my hat somewhere, my toes were frozen, and the skin between my jacket sleeve and glove was stinging, but I had never felt so warm, so wonderful, cradled by him.

"Allie, are you okay?"

I nodded.

"Did you have the breath knocked out of you?"

Not in the sense in which he meant it.

"Say something," he persisted.

"I'm okay."

He looked at my mouth as I spoke. I looked at his—I wanted to take off my gloves and trace the curve of his lips with the tips of my fingers. His head lowered. I lifted one hand and very lightly touched his cheek. He was so close, I could feel his breath.

"Allie?" His voice was soft, his face so near.

Just one kiss, that's all I wanted. A centimeter more and our lips would touch. There was no sky above me, just Ben. All I wanted was Ben.

"Hey! You guys okay?"

Tim. I had completely forgotten about him. I wrenched my head around and saw him about forty feet up the hill, running toward us.

Ben rolled off me. "We're fine," he said, "just fine."

We sat up like two people awakening from a strange dream, then stood up slowly and dusted the snow off ourselves. "Thanks for checking, little brother," Ben said as Tim reached us.

"Some ride!" Tim exclaimed.

"You've got that right." Ben picked up the rope

165

of the sled and started up the hill, followed by Tim. I straggled behind, needing time to recover.

For the rest of the runs Tim rode with either Ben or me. When he wanted to do the hill alone, Ben and I took turns on the remaining sled rather than riding down together. I didn't know what he was thinking, but I was sure I couldn't get that close again without kissing him.

I no longer felt warm—in fact, my frozen toes no longer felt anything—and Tim, having endured a lot of tumbles, was soaked straight through. We finally headed home.

On the way to the Harringtons' house both Ben and I were silent, which allowed me to lapse into dangerous daydreams. How would it have felt, his lips against mine? What would it be like if he wanted me, only me? I imagined us returning to his house after a kiss in the snow. We'd build a fire together, and snuggle in front of the hearth, and—

I should have left out the fireplace part. An image of Sandra on Christmas Eve, sitting by the hearth, her gold hair catching the firelight, her hand resting on Ben's leg, suddenly popped into my mind.

"Allie? Allie?" The real Ben was speaking.

We'd reached the Harringtons' walk, and I saw that Jen and Sam were up on the porch.

"There's something we should talk about," Ben said.

"I think you're in trouble," Tim observed. "That's how he begins whenever he's going to tell you what you've done bad."

"Allie hasn't done anything bad," Ben assured him.

"Yet," I added, laughing nervously. I was afraid Ben had sensed that my feelings ran deep. Now he was worried things had gone too far and wanted to make clear that there was nothing serious between us. He probably thought he needed to set the story straight before I saw Sandra, before I said something that might ruin his plans for just the two of them tomorrow night.

"It's about tomorrow night," he began.

I frowned and said nothing.

"The boat parade at Windhaven that you're going to with Mike, Ford, and Julia. Remember?"

"Oh. Oh, right. What about it?"

"I've been to that parade," Tim interjected. "It's pretty. All the boats have lights. And Santa Claus rides in one."

"I want to make sure you know what you're getting yourself into," Ben said.

I didn't like the tone of his voice, the sound of a big brother warning his little sister.

"I'm not planning to get myself into either a boat or the river, but I can wear a life preserver if you think it's advisable."

"It won't help you in the woods," he replied.

"What do you mean?"

"You're going to Ford's cabin in the woods." His voice cracked with frustration. "And his parents aren't going to be there."

"So?" I challenged him.

"I don't like to stick my nose into other people's business, Allie. But your sisters haven't been here that long, and Julia may not know about the stories Ford likes to tell—the things he brags about to other guys. That cabin is a favorite place for his . . . his . . . conquests."

I laughed at Ben's old-fashioned language. But actually, I'd already thought about the possibility. Aunt Jen had a cabin at Windhaven, a camping area about forty minutes from Thornhill, and I knew most of the dwellings were isolated, surrounded by dense woods. My main reason for saying yes the night before was to make sure that Julia didn't go alone.

"Mike's no angel either," Ben added.

"Excuse me?" Now he was treading on dangerous ground.

"Mike's got a reputation."

"So do you," I reminded him. What a jerk— trying to destroy my thin little hope for romance, my only hope for getting over him!

"Not the same kind of reputation," he replied, his jaws tight.

"What kind do you have?" Tim asked.

Ben glanced down at him. "This conversation is between Allie and me, okay? Dad and Jen are on the porch. Go tell them about sledding."

Tim pretended to start off, then circled back, standing behind Ben, listening. To me, Ben said, "Mike likes to brag about what girl he's been with and what he's done, what *they've* done—"

"You're assuming I'm just another girl to Mike," I said angrily. "You wouldn't want me to assume that Sandra's just another girl to you, would you?"

He turned away.

"What gives you the right—"

"Listen to me," he said, turning back. "Mike's very competitive."

"Like you're not?" I replied.

"Leave me out of this!" Ben exclaimed, color rising in his cheeks.

"I will," I replied, "just as soon as *you* leave *my* life alone!"

Jen and Sam turned, hearing our heated conversation. Tim wasn't going anywhere.

"I'm only looking out for you," Ben told me. "I'm warning you, Allie. Mike is competitive, and since he can't compete in drama and Ford can't compete in sports, they compete with each other in something else."

"What?" Tim asked.

Ben glanced behind him. "Crazy Eights. Scram!"

"Well," I said, "maybe I haven't had as much experience as you and all the other macho guys of Thornhill High, but no guy talks me into anything. I know who I am." *An idiot who has fallen in love with you,* I thought. "And I know what I want. And the last thing I need right now is you acting like my big brother."

"Fine," he said.

"Fine," I said.

We stared at each other, then I turned on my heel and stomped home.

Seventeen

I LOVE THE woods. Add a river and a cabin, and I'm one happy camper. Five P.M. Tuesday, I eagerly pulled on my new hiking boots. Despite Ben's warning I was looking forward to our trip to Windhaven.

Sandra, who was getting ready for her date with Ben, came to my room, hunting for a pair of silver earrings to go with a new outfit. "If you don't mind me giving you a little advice," she said, looking down at my heavy boots, "Mike likes really feminine stuff."

I shrugged. "Okay with me if he wears high-heeled ankle boots."

Julia was in the bathroom, and her laugh echoed out from there. "Can I borrow your old hikers, Allie?"

"Sure. I've got some extra warm socks too."

We needed the wool socks when we reached the docks of Windhaven Marina on the Hudson. The night was clear and very cold. Boats sailed past with thousands of colored lights twinkling in the wind, each boat a starry constellation shining against the black night. Mike stood behind me, his warm arms around me, bending his head close to mine, the two of us oohing and aahing at the passing boats. It was a scene sparkling with romance and possibility; maybe that's what convinced me it was time to give up. As hard as I tried, I still felt nothing for him.

After the parade we returned to the marina lot to pick up backpacks that the guys had stuffed with blankets and snacks.

"I thought we'd leave the car here and take a moonlight hike to the cabin," Ford said as we put on our packs. "It's about a half mile from here."

"Sounds good," I replied. I wished we could hike all night.

Ford led the way, followed by my sister and me, with Mike last in line. The path was winding, but the moonlight guided us, breaking through the leafless branches, glistening on old stumps and sprawling logs that were sugared with snow. The walk would have been perfect if only Ford had shut up. Instead of listening to the gorgeous silences and mysterious night stirrings of wood creatures, we got to hear him talk about himself.

As we walked I noticed that Ford's backpack was coming unzipped. I stared at the shiny cans inside: He had brought a six-pack of beer. "Did you guys bring any sodas?" I asked.

"Lots," Julia said, pointing to Ford's pack, then she saw the beer.

Ford glanced over his shoulder and removed his pack so he could zip it up. I opened mine to check the contents. More beer. "I hope we have soda," I said, "because I don't do alcohol."

"You'll be thirsty when we get to the cabin," Ford replied. "The beer will taste good."

"We're underage," I reminded him.

"Lighten up, Allie," Ford said. "No one's around."

Mike glanced from him to me.

"That's just it," I told Ford. "If we were legal, I still wouldn't drink when I'm in an isolated place with someone I don't know very well."

"She's your date," Ford told Mike. "What was it you said last night—you like a challenge?"

"Excuse me?" I said.

"It's okay, Allie," Mike answered quietly. "I packed one soda. We can split it."

"Three ways?" Julia asked.

"She's your date," Mike told Ford.

"They'll change their minds when we get to the cabin and it feels like a meat freezer," Ford replied.

"Don't count on it," I said.

"You can't just turn up a thermostat," he went on. "It takes a while to build a good fire."

"I know. I was a Girl Scout."

"Still are," Ford remarked. To Julia he said, "My parents keep brandy there. You'll like it. It'll warm you all the way down." He pulled her back against him, running his hand down the front of her.

Before she could react, there was a loud crash in the brush. We all jumped. It sounded like a large animal, a deer maybe, and had come from the path behind us. Ford took advantage of the moment, holding on to Julia tightly, his hands moving over the front of her, sculpting her. I saw her pull forward, trying to loosen his grip.

There was another crashing sound, then a shout. "Allie! Allie, help!"

Tim's voice. For a moment I stood frozen with amazement, then I raced back over the trail. Julia was right behind me, the guys following her.

"Tim, where are you?"

"Over here," he called back to me. "Here."

We found him in a small clearing along with someone else. "Craig!" I said, surprised.

Tim's neighbor was standing on one leg, leaning up against a tree, his hand gripping a low branch. "Hey, guys," Craig greeted us, as if we were passing by in the school cafeteria. "What's up?"

"Are you hurt?" I asked. There was snow all over his jacket, and I noticed he wasn't putting weight on one ankle.

"Just resting," he replied.

"He's hurt. He stepped in a hole," Tim said.

Mike shook his head, his mouth pulling tight in a look of disgust. Then he crouched down and began to probe the sore ankle. Craig winced. "Really, I'm okay," he insisted.

Mike didn't buy it. "I think you've done some damage. You need to get it checked out. Allie, give me your scarf and hold his foot off the ground, will you?"

I knelt down and supported Craig's foot while

Mike bound it in my scarf and his, twisting them around the foot and ankle like bulky athletic wraps. Ford sat down on a log and watched, looking as if he wanted to strangle Craig. Julia remained standing, though Ford had brushed off a wide space on the log for her.

"What are you doing here, Tim?" she asked.

"Um . . ."

"I was taking pictures at the boat parade," Craig answered for the little boy, "and brought Tim along."

Ford narrowed his eyes. "Where's your camera?"

"In the car. I used up all my film."

Mike rested back on his heels, studying his finished work. "It'll do."

"Thanks, Mike," Craig said. "It feels better already. Have a good hike, everyone. Tim and I are heading back to the lot."

But Tim shook his head. "Craig," he said.

"We're leaving, Tim," Craig replied, as gruffly as I'd ever heard him speak. He tried to walk, then stopped and sucked in air. I knew he was in agony.

"Don't put weight on it, stupid!" Mike said sharply.

"Okay. No problem," Craig replied. "You all go ahead with your hike. We're not far from the car. Tim will find me a walking stick, right, Tim?"

The little boy didn't budge.

"Put your arm around me and lean on me," I told Craig. "I'll walk you back."

He refused. "I don't want to ruin your night."

"I find that hard to believe," Ford said with a sarcastic smile. "In fact, I find you hard to believe."

175

"I'll take his other side, Allie," Mike said. "We can move faster."

"I'm sorry about this," Craig told us as we helped him along.

"When you can walk again, I'm going to kill you," Mike replied.

"Why not put me out of my misery now?"

"Because I owe you for some good newspaper photos."

We made our way back to the parking lot. Since Craig's car had a stick shift and clutch, which required him to drive with both feet, Mike had to play chauffeur for Craig and Tim. Julia and I followed them in Ford's car. The six of us met up again at a hospital ER about ten miles from Thornhill. As soon as we arrived I called Sam from a pay phone. He said he'd contact Craig's parents, then come out quickly to take care of matters.

By the time I got back to the group, Craig had been registered and given a wheelchair, so there was nothing for us to do but wait until he could be seen.

"There's no reason for you guys to hang around," Craig told us. "Someone's coming from home."

Ford and Mike glanced up at the clock. A few minutes after eight—there was plenty of time to continue the date.

"I'm staying," I said.

Julia still wasn't talking, but she'd chosen a seat next to me, as if to say, Whatever Allie's doing, I'm doing.

"You know what I'm wondering," Ford said to

Craig, "how come you kept looking our way at the basketball game—at Bingo's too—but won't look at Julia now?"

I wanted to punch him in the nose, but Craig replied calmly, "It's a standard reaction when you've made a fool of yourself."

"It's a standard reaction when you're really hot for a girl you can't have," Ford said.

Craig met his eyes straight on.

"If I didn't know better," Ford persisted, "I'd think you were following us tonight."

"We were," Tim volunteered, "to make sure Allie and Julia were okay."

"What?" Mike said. "Why?"

"Ben told Allie that she shouldn't go because Ford did things in his cabin," Tim replied. "He said you would too, Mike, because you're repetitive."

"Competitive," I corrected quietly.

Mike, Julia, and Ford turned to me—Ford with a look of disbelief.

"That's what happens when you go around bragging," I said.

"Allie wanted to go anyway," Tim continued. "And Ben wouldn't come with me to make sure she was okay. So I asked Craig because he was going to take pictures of the parade."

"Allie," Julia said accusingly, "how come you never mentioned any of this to me?"

I shrugged. "I figured it was just stories. Besides, I knew we could take care of ourselves."

Ford swore softly under his breath. Mike looked

uneasy. Craig focused on the registration desk, his mouth set in a grim line. Julia watched him for a minute, then rested her chin in her hands, her fingers covering her face up to her eyes.

That's how Ben found our cheerful little group. He and Sandra had been sent to the hospital while Sam tried to contact Craig's parents.

Ford was the first to see Ben. "Thanks," he said sarcastically. "Thanks a lot."

Ben looked uncertainly from one person to the next. "Tim, what were you and—"

"You wouldn't come with me," Tim cried defensively. "I asked you to, but you said Allie's friends were none of our business."

"Oh, jeez," Ben murmured, figuring out the situation. "What a mess I've made."

Ben took charge then, saying he'd stay with Craig and Tim. Julia looked as if she were going to cry and asked Ford to take her home.

"Me too," I said.

"And me," Sandra chimed in. "Hospitals are so depressing." She was the only one in a cheerful mood. "I just don't know how anyone stands them."

"People don't come here to have a good time," I snapped.

She shrugged and a few minutes later squeezed in Ford's car, seating herself between Mike and me. Sandra and Mike talked all the way home, though what they said, I wasn't sure and didn't care.

My mind was on Craig . . . and Julia and Ben and me, and what a huge mess we'd made.

Eighteen

SANDRA THOUGHT IT was extraordinarily lucky that we'd come across Craig when he was injured. I didn't enlighten her. Julia said nothing that night until I met her in the bathroom. She was brushing her teeth fiercely.

"Want to talk?" I asked.

She showed me a mouth full of foam.

"I guess I should've warned you."

She spit into the sink and rinsed. "You guess right."

"I—I guess I didn't want it to be true," I explained.

"So you could prove a point to Ben? So you could be out while he was out?"

Her words hit home.

"I'm sorry, Al," she said quickly. "I'm mad, and I'm all mixed up."

"Mad at me? At Ford?"

"At both of you—and myself. I must've been crazy when I decided to date him."

"I hope Craig's doing all right."

"Me too," she said, but volunteered nothing more.

The next morning I called Craig's house and left a message for him to call back when he was up to it. Then my sisters and I were corralled by my mother for a major housecleaning event. At lunch Sandra asked to borrow my car so she could go shopping.

"You mean there's still an outfit in the mall you haven't tried on?"

She grinned at me. "If there is, I'm going to find it."

As soon as Sandra left, Julia started practicing piano. She was playing up a storm and didn't hear the light knock at the back door.

"Hey, Craig," I said as I opened the door. "How are you doing?"

"Good." He leaned on a pair of crutches. "Good."

"I can see that," I said. "Tell me, are you slowly turning into a mummy, or is that a new-style boot?"

He laughed. "The foot's broken, but not too bad."

"Come on in."

"I won't stay long," he said, hobbling into the kitchen.

"Does it still hurt?" I asked.

He shook his head. "They gave me lots of painkillers."

"Yeah? Do they work for the heart too?"

"Not so far," he said, sitting on the edge of a

high stool. "I'm really sorry about last night, Allie. I came to apologize."

"You don't owe me an apology," I replied. "Ford had those backpacks loaded with beer. I was just as glad to get home."

He nodded. "I'd hoped that something good would come out of it for you. I thought maybe you'd stay at the hospital so you could have some time with Ben."

"Why would I want time with Ben?"

He just looked at me.

"I'm that obvious, huh?"

"Maybe I can see it because I'm in the same boat." He set his crutches aside, then pulled off his backpack. "I brought Julia's pictures," he said, reaching into the sack. "Double prints, one envelope for her and one for you in case you want to take some photos back to school. In your envelope I added pictures of Sandra and Tim . . . and Ben. Okay?"

"It's the best present you could give me," I told him. "Thanks."

He glanced toward the living room, where the piano music was reaching a crescendo. "I also bought a pair of tickets to the opera for Julia."

"I'll go get her."

"Allie, wait!" he said. "Would you stay around when I apologize to her? I feel like a real jerk."

"I'll stay," I promised, "but you are *not* a jerk."

I hurried off and caught my sister at a half-note pause. "Got a minute?" I asked. "Craig's in the kitchen."

Julia's hands hovered above the keys. "Craig?"

She got up and bumped into a leg of the piano, which was unlike her. As we passed through the hall I saw her glance at herself in the mirror and tuck up a piece of hair. There was hope.

"Oh, no!" she said as soon as she saw Craig's cast.

He gave her a crooked smile. "It's no big deal. And I won't stay long. I just wanted to apologize."

"For what?" she asked.

"Screwing up your date last night. Making Ford mad. Embarrassing you. Acting like an idiot. Did I leave anything out?"

"No big deal," she repeated back to him.

"I thought you might like to have these," he told her, handing over the pictures. "They're from the fall production. I'd be glad to make more if you want to give some to Ford."

"Thanks," she said, and opened the envelope.

I peered over her shoulder. Ben was right about the photos: The picture on top was more than a snapshot of a pretty face. Craig had caught the energy and spirit of Julia. She pulled out another photo, one he'd taken backstage before she went on. You could see her excitement, the effort to focus, the fear and the hope, all bundled inside her.

"This is wonderful!" I said, taking it from her, holding it up for Craig.

He nodded and smiled. "It's my favorite. Used a telephoto."

Julia slid the pictures back in the envelope. "I want to look at these by myself if you don't mind."

"Sure, I've got to get going anyway," Craig

replied, pulling on his backpack. "One other thing: I have two tickets to a concert given by the Hudson Valley Opera Company on New Year's Eve."

Julia's eyes opened wide. "New Year's Eve?"

He nodded and reached into his pocket. "The company is local, but I think they're good. And it's early in the evening, so I thought you and Ford could fit it in before Twist's party."

"Oh," she said, sounding disappointed.

"I can't fix last night," he explained. "I hope these will make up for it in some way." He handed her the tickets and pulled himself up on his crutches.

Julia gazed up at him with her round green eyes, standing close to him so he had to bend his head to look down at her. I'd seen that ploy before.

"The problem is," she said, "the only kind of operas Ford knows are soaps. I think he'd be disappointed."

"Well, I was trying to find something you'd like. It's the thought that counts."

"So you don't want to go?" she said, sweeping him with her long lashes.

"I'm sure somebody will enjoy the concert," Craig replied. "Maybe Allie and you could go together," he suggested, "then meet up with . . . whoever, I don't know. I'm not good at these things."

Julia flicked the tickets back and forth against one wrist, then rested her hand on Craig's. "I thought *you* liked this kind of music. You said the company was good."

"I like all kinds," he replied, swinging himself toward the door as soon as she removed her hand. "And this company really is talented. Well, I've got to return my father's car. He doesn't like to drive my stick."

Julia watched him hobble out onto the porch, then hurried after him and grabbed his crutches from behind. "I'm *not* letting go," she said.

Craig looked over his shoulder at her, surprised.

"Want me to hold up a sign?" she asked, frustrated. "Come on, Craig, I was hinting for you to ask me out."

"When?" he asked.

She blinked, then burst out laughing. "Turn around," she said, letting go of one crutch. "Please?"

He faced her, looking uncertain.

"I was rude when I didn't call you back," Julia told him. "Rude and wrong about you."

He studied her face as if she were speaking a foreign language.

"I'm sorry, and I'm asking for another chance. Okay? What time is the concert?"

"Seven."

"Ask me, Craig! Ask me if I'm doing anything New Year's Eve! I know it's stupid and old-fashioned, but I'm one of those girls who likes to be asked out by the guy."

"I like being invited by the girl," he replied.

Julia chewed a finger, looking nervous.

Craig's eyes crinkled a little, a shy smile forming on his face. "Want to go out on New Year's Eve?" he asked.

"Yes."

Can the way two people look at each other really be equal to a kiss? Their lingering gaze was. I quietly closed the back door and retreated to the family room, figuring it would be a while before Craig's father got his car back.

That look haunted me all day—the long gaze between a girl and a guy who were falling in love. That night I tossed and turned, barely sleeping. Having seen the real thing, I knew I couldn't fake it anymore.

And I couldn't face all those parties. I'd come to like some of my sisters' friends, like Janice and Caroline, but a night of partying with the fast crowd and pretending with Mike was not the way I wanted to start the new year. Julia told me that she'd delivered the bad news to Ford as soon as Craig went home Wednesday. Thursday it was my turn. Unlike Ford, however, Mike wasn't a bad guy, and I felt like a louse backing out the morning of New Year's Eve. But he took the news pretty well. When I called Mike to explain, he interrupted my long apology and said, "It's okay, Allie, I understand. Don't worry about it." I was thankful that he didn't give me a hard time.

My mother, on the other hand, was not pleased. Just when she thought her duckling was turning into a swan, I announced I was staying home on *the* big party-and-date night.

"Wish I could stay home," was all my father said.

An hour later, when everyone was out on errands,

Aunt Jen showed up, dressed as if she'd just left work, offering no explanation except a sudden impulse to "visit."

"This is about tonight, isn't it?" I asked suspiciously. "Did my mother call you?"

"Your father."

"Traitor!"

"He says the two of us are alike."

"Well, if we are," I replied, "then you know there are times when you're happiest by yourself. Cripe, *he* knows that!"

She held up a white box tied in string. "I stopped at a bakery. It's almost lunch. Want to add inches to our waistline and talk a little?"

"No."

She slipped off the string and opened the box. I surveyed the pastries.

"Oh, why not," I said. We started with two crullers and an account of what had happened at Windhaven. I guess I repeated myself a couple of times.

"I think I've got the part about Julia, Craig, and true love," Aunt Jen finally told me, wiping some powdered sugar from her mouth. "What's really on your mind?"

Ben. He'd been on my mind since the day we met.

"Want me to guess?" she asked.

I glanced away.

"Ben Harrington," she said. "What went wrong between you two? Something was very right when you started."

I could feel the tears building up. "I went wrong."

"What do you mean?"

"I realized it yesterday. I was watching Craig and saw how he kept missing his opportunities. He was so sure he didn't have a chance that he couldn't see it—not even when Julia was batting her eyes at him like a pair of butterflies in distress. It got me thinking. I had a chance with Ben, but I didn't go for it. I let Sandra take over—I didn't even try."

My aunt nodded.

"The thing is, in sports and academics I'm a fighter. But I got myself so wrapped up in who was in what crowd and how a guy could be interested in me when my cool and beautiful sisters were around—I just wimped out."

"Now and then we all wimp out," Aunt Jen said.

"Yes, but I . . ."

She waited patiently for me to go on.

". . . think I love him. I couldn't help it—I fell for him." I tried to blink back the tears; it was useless. "Picked a great time to wimp out, didn't I? I know, I know, I'm young, and there are other sea horses in the ocean."

Aunt Jen smiled and touched my cheek gently. "I think you mean starfish in the sea."

"I wish I'd stop wanting him so much. And I wish I hadn't been such an idiot."

"Allie, one thing I know about love is that you can't love another person well until you love yourself. Both of you have to believe you have a lot to offer each other. I think you do believe in yourself now. Next time you get a chance at love, you'll be ready."

"Will it be as good as I think it could have been for Ben and me?"

"Oh, just you wait, girl," she said, smiling, "just you wait!" She gave me a hug.

"You brides," I teased her, "you're all so starry-eyed."

"Maybe . . . maybe. As for tonight, how does this suit you?" She held up a string, dangling a key.

"Your cabin?" I said, reaching for the key. "I can finish that moonlight hike and test out my new sleeping bag. I'd love it."

"You mother will worry that it's too lonely for you."

"I've camped by myself plenty of times," I assured her, swinging the key on its string. "My father will talk her into it—after you talk him into it."

She laughed.

"Happy New Year," I said, smiling through my tears.

"Happy new you."

Nineteen

M Y MOTHER PACKED a freezer chest full of my favorite food. My father carried it out to the car and checked the battery on my cellular phone. It was their way of parenting, and I appreciated the fact that they did those things instead of asking a lot of questions.

I was sorry I wouldn't see Julia and Craig dressed up for the concert that evening. I was glad, however, to miss Sandra's New Year's Eve outfit, which I knew would be breathtaking. I was on the road by four o'clock and arrived at the cabin at sunset.

For a long time I stood outside and watched the sky give its last amazing color show of the year. Then after a quick dinner I went for an evening walk. I thought a lot about Ben and wondered what it would be like to take a moonlit hike with him. I remembered every second of our almost-kiss in the snow and found myself close to tears again, hanging on desperately to Aunt Jen's wisdom. *Next time,* I thought. *I know myself better now. Next time I'll be ready.* Though how there could be a time when I'd love anyone but Ben, I sure didn't know.

It was only eight-thirty when I got back to Jen's place, but I was tired. I lugged armloads of wood inside the one-room cabin, stoked up the fire, and put on my Fields Follies nightshirt. The shirt, which was left over from our senior class performance, reached to midthigh and was decorated with glitter and tiny feathers in pink, purple, and orange. I pulled on the leopard slippers Tim had given me, laughing at my New Year's Eve outfit. With my sleeping bag unzipped and spread out in front of the hearth and the lights extinguished so I could enjoy the flickering fire, I took out a new paperback romance and lay down to read.

I didn't make it past page eight. At least, that's what page I found myself facedown on when I awoke some time later. I jerked up, having been startled by a noise, though my head was too foggy to recall clearly what I'd heard. Snow sliding off the roof, I told myself. The fire was nearly out, and the room was chilly. I rose to put on a log, then heard another noise: crunching snow, footsteps outside the cabin.

As if the person knew I was listening, the footsteps stopped. I waited in the silence, barely breathing. Maybe I'd imagined the steps; maybe it was just another moonlight hiker.

I tiptoed over to the window and peered through the heavy curtains. My skin prickled.

From that angle I couldn't see anyone, but a car was parked out front—one I didn't recognize. My Audi was around back. I wondered if I could slip out the front door, which was the only door to the place, and run around the cabin to my car. No—better to exit through the back window. The tiny back window? *Calm down, Allie.* This was just another camper, maybe someone who was lost, I told myself. But I was scared. Remembering I'd left my cellular phone on the kitchen counter close to the door, I hurried to get it. I was about to punch 911, then realized that by the time the police found a cabin in Windhaven, I could be wearing an ax in my back.

Just then the door handle rattled. I watched in disbelief as someone standing on the other side of the door turned the knob. The door remained bolted closed; though Aunt Jen rarely locked up in the country, I had done so that night.

Then I heard metal scraping inside metal. How easy would it be to pick the old lock?

I reached for the only weapon close by—a big iron skillet that hung above the stove. I stood back against the wall, my arms raised, ready to come down hard on the intruder.

The lock clicked, and the door swung open.

"Ben!"

"Allie!"

We stared at each other for a long moment, then he said, "Could you lower that thing?"

I dropped the skillet to my side, feeling foolish

and suddenly angry, having been frightened for no reason. "What are you doing here?"

"I was going to ask the same thing of you."

"I was given a key."

"So was I," he said in a voice as icy as mine.

Then his eyes traveled down me, noticing the glittery nightshirt, my long bare legs, and the big leopard slippers.

"You're supposed to be out celebrating," I told him. "Sandra will be waiting for you. She's spent the whole week putting together an incredible outfit."

"I think yours wins the prize," Ben replied, one side of his mouth drawing up.

My cheeks burned, and I quickly walked away from him.

He followed me. "Listen, I'm sorry," he said, "but Jen and my father never mentioned you might be here."

"*Might* be? She *knew* I was! I can't believe she tried to fix things this way!"

"I honestly didn't know you were here, Allie," he said, then leaned down and picked up my paperback. "You read these kinds of books?"

I snatched the romance away from him. "You had to see smoke coming out of the chimney. You had to know someone was inside."

"I was thinking about . . . other things. I didn't even see your Audi, much less chimney smoke."

"And furthermore," I said, as if I'd caught him in some kind of trick, "that's not your car."

"It's my father's. I lent mine to Craig since he needed an automatic."

I tossed down the book. "When I see Aunt Jen," I muttered to myself.

"What was she trying to fix?" he asked.

I glanced up at him, and his dark brown eyes held mine. Would there ever be a time when he looked in my eyes and I didn't feel as if I were falling under his spell? I looked down quickly at my furry feet. I'd rather have taken a double set of exams than answer his one question. But I knew if I wanted to move on and be ready for the next time, I had to be straight with him.

"Aunt Jen knows I, uh, kind of . . . sort of . . . fell for you. Big time." My voice was shaking. "Of course, you're used to that. Anyway, I missed my chance with you, and she was trying to give me another. That's all."

I felt his hands on my shoulders. "Allie, look at me," he said.

"Thanks, but I've looked enough."

He cupped my face in his hands, lifting it up until I had to meet his eyes. "Here's what I'm not used to: waking up able to think of nothing but seeing one girl. Going to sleep, thinking about that girl. Hoping that when I turn a corner, that girl will be there. Driving and hoping like crazy every time I see a silver car go by. Listening for anything anyone—including her sister who I'm supposed to be dating—might say about the girl. Cheering at a basketball game, aware of every time the girl brushes against me. Being jealous of a seven-year-old kid when the girl puts her arms around him. That's what I can't get used to. Big time."

With one finger he gently traced the shape of my mouth. "I was just trying to survive the holiday," he said. "I never expected to fall in love."

"You too?"

"I love you, Allie."

He cradled my head, and his lips touched mine. There was sweet fire in them, and it swept straight through me. I started to tremble. His arms came around me and pulled me close. We held on tight to each other, and he rocked me a little. "I can't believe you're actually in my arms," he said, "and that you want to be. I'd stopped hoping."

I pulled back my head and reached up to touch his face. "I want to be. You don't know how much!"

I could feel his heart beating fast beneath his jacket. He pulled my face toward his, and we started kissing again. Then the phone rang, making both of us jump.

"It's my cellular."

We watched it from across the room, staying wrapped in each other's arms. "I guess I'd better answer it," I told him. He let go of me, and I hurried over to pick it up.

"You had me worried," Aunt Jen said before I spoke a word.

"Well, you should be," I replied into the phone. "Because a few minutes ago I was ready to kill you—right after I nearly walloped Ben on the head with your skillet."

"You didn't."

"Came close," I said, laughing. "Who do you think you are? Cupid?"

"It wasn't planned," Aunt Jen explained. "It just evolved after your mother called in a panic saying Ben had broken his date with Sandra."

"Sandra! I forgot! It's New Year's. She'll never speak to me again."

"She's out with Mike, according to the latest bulletin from your father. You girls are making your parents crazy."

Ben was standing next to me now. "Sandra's out with Mike," I told him.

"I counted on that," he said.

"Anyway, dearest niece," my aunt went on, "I'm calling to warn you that Sam, Tim, and I are on our way with our sleeping bags."

"First you play Cupid, now you're a chaperon."

"Exactly."

We signed off, and I told Ben they were on their way. "I suppose I should change out of my sparkles and feathers."

He laughed. "Before you do, let's dance."

I glanced around the cabin. "All I brought was a disc player with headphones."

"Who needs music?" he asked.

"Not me," I replied, smiling. "I proved that once before."

He took off his jacket and wrapped it around my shoulders, holding me warm in his arms. Then we danced slowly to what had become "our song," the music we heard inside us.

Do you ever wonder about falling in love? About members of the opposite sex? Do you need a little friendly advice but have no one to turn to? Well, that's where we come in . . . Jenny and Jake. Send us those questions you're dying to ask, and we'll give you the straight scoop on life and love in the nineties.

DEAR JAKE

Q: *My boyfriend, Pete, never pays much attention to me when we're in school. When we go out on the weekends, though, he's great. What's going on? Is he embarrassed to be seen with me?*

RK, Plainfield, NJ

A: There are several possible explanations for Pete's behavior. Maybe he's unsure of how to treat you around his or your friends. He could be shy about showing his affection in front of people who could tease him later, or he could feel awkward around your friends if he doesn't know them too well. It could be that Pete's very focused on his studies and doesn't want to be distracted while he's in school. Basically you're going to have to confront the guy if you want a straight answer. Try to pose the question without any anger or resentment—that could put him into a defensive mode. Instead let him know that you're feeling hurt and wondering why he doesn't talk to you much during the week. Once you know what's motivating his silent treatment, you can work on a compromise that will make you both happy.

Q: *My ex-boyfriend Aaron is dating other girls, but he doesn't like that I'm dating other guys. He's told all his friends not to go out with me even though one of them, Jason, likes me. I don't want to hurt Aaron because I do still care about him, but shouldn't I be able to date anyone I want to?*

AT, Des Moines, Iowa

A: Even if Aaron decided to join a monastery and never date again, the fact that you two are broken up means that he has no say in your current dating life. He's trying to control you, and that's not okay. It's understandable that you still worry about his feelings, but you have to put yourself first. Aaron has no right to tell other people that they *can't* date you or to tell you that other guys are off-limits. However, you did mention that Jason is a friend of Aaron's, and that can be a dangerous area. Would you want Aaron to go out with one of your close friends? I'm guessing no. If you and Jason have a real connection that you think could lead to something serious, don't give up on it. But if it's just a crush, try to find someone who isn't friends with Aaron so you can truly have a fresh start.

DEAR JENNY

Q: *I decided to break up with my boyfriend, Steve, but then he found out his parents are getting divorced. He's going through such an awful time that I can't imagine hurting him, but I just don't want to be with him anymore. What do I do?*

PH, Oxford, MI

A: Your motives are very kind—you want to spare Steve additional pain. However, what you're doing will actually make things worse for him in the long run. Eventually you'll have to be honest, and the news will hurt a lot more after you've been together for even longer. Watching your parents separate is really tough, and it can take a lot of energy to stay strong. What Steve needs now is your support. Tell him that while your romantic feelings have changed and you no longer want to be his girlfriend, you do want to be there for him as a friend. Instead of being the girl who stuck around out of pity and then ditched him once the divorce was final, you'll be the one who never lied to him and helped him through a rough time without making false promises.

Q: *I have a major crush on the son of my mom's best friend. When he comes to our house with his mom, he always flirts a lot, but he's a couple of years older than me, and I can't tell if he's just teasing or if he really likes me. How can I find out without making a fool of myself in front of someone I'll have to see all the time?*

TH, Jackson, TN

A: I know exactly how you feel—when I was thirteen, my mom had this friend with a gorgeous, incredible son who I would have died to go out with. I never told him how I felt, and I always wondered what would have happened. Like you, I was afraid of the potential embarrassment factor of being turned down by someone who knew my *mom*.

But you know what? I never realized that there are ways to be subtle in these situations. So I advise you to do what I should have done—go for it. Flirt back, encourage his interest, and try to talk to him alone, without your parents around. It can be tempting when you like a guy to get supershy around him, but you must do the opposite and be your friendliest. This should give him the opportunity to know that you're interested and to give you more information about how he feels.

Do you have questions about love? Write to:
Jenny Burgess or Jake Korman
c/o Daniel Weiss Associates
33 West 17th Street
New York, NY 10011

Don't miss any of the books in *Love Stories*
—the romantic series from Bantam Books!